THE LUGGAGE DROP

A NOVEL

STACY A. KING

LUCKY DIMES MEDIA, LLC

THE LUGGAGE DROP

Copyright © 2019 by Stacy A. King

All rights reserved.

Published in the United States of America by Lucky Dimes Media, LLC

10524 Moss Park Rd. Ste 204-629
Orlando, FL 32832

Cover design and interior by ebooklaunch.com

Library of Congress Control Number: 2018914602

ISBN: 978-0-578-43040-9

To my four superheroes

BOOMERANG

"No!" she screams while the song "Apologize" by Ryan Tedder pours from the speakers of her Jeep radio. But the mere one syllable word is no rival for the inevitable and collides with a sickening *THUD*. Within the small space of the moving four-by-four, the song continues to play.

Alone at the wheel, she cries out, "Damn it!" as she maneuvers her right foot from the gas pedal to the brake pedal and then back again and re-accelerates the engine. With bumper to bumper traffic zipping by, and no place to pull over, she steadies the steering wheel with both hands, keeps the Jeep in her lane and applies steady pressure to the gas pedal. Out of frustration, she hits the steering wheel with her fist and mutters, "What the hell? Where'd that come from?"

Shaken by what just happened, her vocal utterances turn inward while she drives with the flow of traffic as if nothing happened. *How am I going to tell her I killed a bird? She loves birds. I hope it wasn't a blue barn swallow. They've always been her favorite.* And she continues to drive along a busy sunlit interstate in America's heartland oblivious to the song playing on the radio.

An hour later, as she applies the brakes while pulling into an Oklahoma suburban driveway that leads to a single-story brick French Country style house, she hears a high-pitched squeal. As she brings the Jeep Wrangler to a complete stop, she groans and blurts out, "I thought we replaced you? Damn brake pads."

In turn, a ratcheting sound rings out as she yanks the emergency brake back. She then turns the radio dial to the off position and turns the engine off. With disappointment and sadness tainting her voice, she pulls the key out of the ignition switch and murmurs, "I wanted to surprise her. And now I have a dead bird in the grill...a dead bird."

After a brief pause, she opens the driver's side door and slips out of the Jeep. And as she closes the door behind her, curiosity propels her toward the front of the vehicle. An intoxicating distant smell of wood smoke and burning leaves carried by a gentle wind mingles in the breezy Indian summer day air and fills her nasal passageways while she walks with caution toward the unknown. After two tentative steps forward, she reaches the front tire on the driver's side of the rig. Then, as her right foot comes into contact with the cement driveway beneath her feet, she hears a frantic *FLAP! FLAP! FLAP!*

Shocked by what she hears, she freezes. *No way. It can't be.* Unable to resist the urge to look, she breaks free from her frozen stance and slinks around the corner of the Jeep. As she turns the corner, curiosity mixed with the promise of life—like an invisible magnetic force—pushes her toward the stainless steel grill. As she bends forward, she sees the forked steel blue tail of a swallow sticking out of the grill. Startled by what she's looking at, her jade green eyes pop wide open, and she gasps while taking a step back and covering her mouth with both hands. As she does, she hears a frenzied *FLAP...FLAP... WHOOSH!* And a bird, the size of a lemon, with a fluffy tawny colored belly, cobalt blue wings and cinnamon-colored throat, bursts out of the grill. "Huh?" she says shaking her head.

The little blue bird—looking unscathed—sings as it gains momentum and lift. With her hands now about an inch from her mouth, she says, with renewed hope emanating from her voice, "Fly little bird! Fly! Go home! Your mommy's calling for you!" And she shakes her head once again astonished at what she's witnessing. A smile spreads across her face, and she exhales. Her hands drop away from her mouth, and her tense shoulders relax like a piece of wax melting in a warming pot as she watches the bird drift off into the watery blue sky.

As the bird disappears, she turns her attention back to the Jeep and mouths, "Wow!" She then walks to the back of the sports utility vehicle to get her belongings. When she gets to the Jeep tailgate, she notices fiery red-orange leaves from a young maple tree in the front yard, and about ten feet from the driveway, floating in the unrestrained space around it.

The maple tree, from which the leaves fall, is a lone tree on a half-acre lot in a neighborhood outside of Oklahoma City. And like all the other colorful maple trees planted throughout the rural modern housing development, it looks out-of-place standing there with the brittle brown, tumbleweed ridden Oklahoma landscape in the background. And though it stands alone, on this particular lot, its shedding leaves have completely caught her attention, and she's mesmerized by them.

After staring at the leaves, she looks away from the tree, opens the back of the four-by-four, collects her luggage and then pulls the tinted hard top rear window down. She then closes the tailgate door and pushes, with the weight from the right side of her body, against the door. As she hears the door latch click into place, she looks again at the leaves and then at the vulnerable-looking tree and says, "You're all alone. Hmm...you sure remind me of myself these last few years." And then, she steps forward, away from the Jeep.

As the free-floating leaves descend toward their final resting place on earth's warm autumn floor, a gust of wind blows several of the leaves onto the sidewalk that runs alongside the house. And when they touch the concrete, and relax into place, they become further displaced by the shuffle of her brown leather cowboy boots. And they swirl around her.

Jen, the woman wearing these cowboy boots, is a middle-aged woman who defines herself as a wife, a mother and a grandmother. And at the moment, she's trying to avoid stepping on the unsettled leaves dancing around her feet as she walks toward the front door of the house. In an odd way, as she dodges the leaves, her behavior makes sense. Just like she shies away from stepping on the leaves, she shies away from the fact that she's a famous American playwright best known for creating the Broadway musical smash hit *Laced* five years ago.

Even stranger than shying away from success, Jen vanished when she found herself swept up into the limelight. And today, she doesn't look like a famous playwright. Instead, she looks like an Oklahoma cowgirl wearing faded blue jeans and a red tank top with long silver hair pulled up in a tight ponytail. And with each step she takes, the fall breeze tugs and pulls at each delicate, time-ridden strand as her ponytail bobs up and down.

As she continues to walk toward the front door, she squeezes the aged luggage handles of four hard shell vintage suitcases. She grips with her left hand the leather handles of two well-traveled mid-size caramel brown leather suitcases adorned with tarnished brass hardware. And she grips with her right hand the ivory leather handle of a toaster size ivory leather cosmetic train case also adorned with brass hardware. The toaster size case bounces along on top of another suitcase, a case with a plastic handle she has a death grip on. It's a case hidden behind the train case. And even though it's somewhat hidden, it stands out amongst the other luggage with its beige fiberboard body, turquoise green leather capped corners, turquoise green plastic handle and chrome hardware.

As she walks toward the front of the house, looking to see if anyone is home, she leans to the left and then to the right. Without warning, a bronze full view glass storm door bursts open, and a woman, who looks like she could be her older sister, yells with uncontrollable excitement in her voice,

"Oh, my God! Jen! Jen! You've come home!" Jen's face lights up with a smile as she walks toward her doppelganger: a near physical double, with dark brown eyes, who looks like a photograph of an awestruck fan framed by the doorway.

Jen's double throws her arms open, leans in toward Jen, and embraces her with all her might. Jen—with a white knuckle grip on the luggage handles—stands still caught up in the woman's grasp, a woman who now has tears streaming down her ageless face. As the woman continues to hold on to Jen, as if she's losing Jen to the current of an ocean riptide, Jen says, "Mom? Do you remember that time when you told me I'd find a place to put it?"

Her mom, loosening her snug grip—but not letting go—says, "Yes."

Jen whispers, "I found it." She then takes a deep breath in and then lets out a sigh of relief. As her lungs fill back up with air, she repeats, "I found it."

As Jen relaxes, in her mother's embrace, she unconsciously loosens the now sweaty grasp she has on each luggage handle. As she does, the luggage handles slip from her grip and dangle from her fingertips. And then gravity—as if it were a baggage room attendant collecting Jen's luggage—takes over and pulls the luggage handles from her hands, and her white knuckles turn flesh pink once again as each old and rugged piece of luggage hits the concrete slab.

One piece of luggage, the beige case with the turquoise decorative detail—now out of Jen's reach—breaks open. And a thick multi-page document, bound at the top by a jumbo black binder clip, falls out of the case. Out of nowhere, a greedy wind gust grabs and rips at the clipped papers. The sturdy binder clip isn't strong enough to fend off the hungry gust, and one piece of flailing paper gives way to the sudden onslaught of wind. The piece of paper disappears as if a hand reached through an invisible barrier and ripped it from the document.

Jen's mom, with eyes full of shock, lets out a gasp and releases her hold on Jen while the remaining papers flutter in the unforgiving wind. She then yells, "Get inside!"

Jen, ignoring her mom's plea, looks at the ground. She then drops to her knees on the gritty concrete slab below to gather her strewn belongings. The first item she rescues from the unexpected microburst is the quivering stack of papers next to the beige case. As her fingertips from her right hand touch the clipped stack of papers and pick them up, the burst of wind stops almost as soon as it started. With her left hand, she grabs the beige case while at the same time she slides the papers back inside. She then grabs hold of the top of the case with both hands—and as darkness once again threatens to envelope the contents as she closes it—she pauses. As she does, she says out loud, "It was locked." She then notices something different about the document. But with no time to lose, she closes the case. *Kuh click. Kuh click.*

THE HOLDING PATTERN

With her hands full of luggage once again, and her mom standing inside the foyer holding the door open for her, Jen walks through the open doorway. As she crosses the threshold, while looking at the ground beneath her feet, she walks right into something. "Whoops!" she chuckles as she looks up at the familiar person who's blocking her from entering the house any further: a man—who looks like he could be Sam Elliot's brother—with medium length, salt and pepper hair and a matching mustache.

In a deep, husky voice, he says, "Well…hello, Jen! I like how ya make an entrance. I heard the commotion and thought I'd check on your mom, and here ya are. What a surprise! You okay? And Maura? You okay too?"

"Yes! Can you believe your eyes?" Maura says.

Before Jack can respond to Maura, Jen says, "Dad! It's so good to see you. How weird. A gust of wind came out of nowhere!"

Her dad reaches out his hands to take her luggage. "Yep…that's Oklahoma for ya. Give me your luggage. I'll put it in the guest room for ya."

"No…that's okay, Dad. I'll get it. Just show me where to go. It's been awhile since I've been here."

"Yeah. It has been awhile. Gosh…last time I saw you here, we had just bought the property."

Jen, nodding in agreement, says, "That's when *Laced* took off on Broadway! Is the guest room to the left?"

"Yep! Follow me, honey."

Jen looks at her mom, who's closing the front door, and says, "I'll be right back!"

Jen's mom motions with her hand, as if she's giving the air a high five and says, "Oh, honey. Go put your things away. I'll see you in a minute. No rush."

"Okay," Jen says with a smile.

She then follows close behind her dad while her mom walks the opposite direction toward the kitchen. As Jen and her dad walk down a narrow hallway, and get closer to the guestroom, she hears from a distance, "Jen? Do you want a cup of coffee?"

"Are you kidding me, Mom?" Jen yells from the hallway. "Did you forget whose kid I am?" she says, laughing.

"You're just like your mama!" Jen's mom shouts from the other end of the house, sounding like a giddy teenager.

Before Jen can respond to her mom's comment, her dad motions with his hand and says, "So there's the guestroom. Put your stuff wherever ya want. You're home now, kiddo."

"Ah…thanks, Dad," Jen says with a smile as she walks past her dad and into the guest room with the luggage handles still tight within her grip, and in the same fashion as when she arrived at her parent's property minutes earlier.

While she's looking around the room—with hands full of luggage—her dad walks up to her, wraps his arms around her, and gives her a hug while saying, "You have no idea how much this means to your mom."

After he releases his embrace, Jen says, "I know…I'm looking forward to catching up after all these years. I have a surprise for her, and there's something we need to discuss. I've missed her, Dad, so much. Are…are you feeling okay?" Jen asks, as her dad grimaces and grabs at the left side of his chest.

"I'm okay," he says as he regains his composure. "I've been feeling a little under the weather. But…I'll be all right. I'll leave ya alone so you can get set up the way you want."

"Wait! Dad! You look like you're in pain…and you're sweating something awful!"

"It's okay. I told ya, I'll be all right. It's gone now."

Jen relents. "Okay. We will talk about this though. I'll be right out."

As Jen's dad leaves the room, and walks toward the kitchen, she can hear her mom yell, "I poured you a cup of coffee, Jen!"

With her mom's voice fading away, Jen releases the security blanket like grip she has on the luggage and sets each case down on the dark hardwood floor. As she does, she notices a rustic pine bench at the end of the bed. *Whoa! Look at these dents and marks. I don't remember this?* She picks up the caramel brown suitcases and sets them down on the bench, side by side. *Kinda looks like they belong here.*

Next, she picks up the cosmetic train case and takes it to the attached guest bathroom and places it on the counter. *Hmm…and this looks like it belongs here too. It fits right in with Mom's rustic décor.* She then saunters back to the guestroom where the last piece of luggage sits, unprotected.

The reflection of the afternoon sun shining through the bedroom window catches Jen's attention as it bounces off the turquoise green plastic handle of the unique piece of luggage. She picks up the case and lays it on the bed. Then she pulls off her cowboy boots and sits down on the edge of the bed. As she does, she positions the case so it now sits in front of her. *How did it break open? Did the locks break? Hmm…*She pulls a small key from her pocket—a key secured to an old and worn piece of faded pink ribbon—and inserts it into the button keyhole on the left side of the case. She tries to turn it, but it doesn't budge. *Hmm…*She pulls the key out of the keyhole and inserts it into the button keyhole on the right side of the case. And again, when she tries to turn the key, it doesn't budge. *Damn. They broke. I guess I won't be locking it again.* She then slides the key back in her pocket.

A dull *kuh click...kuh click...*can be heard as she presses the two broken button locks inward and the latches flip open. "At least I can still close it and open it," she says out loud to herself. She then opens the case, pulls the document out and lays it on the bed. Right away, she sees a gap within the bound papers, a gap she noticed earlier when she put the document back in the case after it fell out during the microburst. Upon further investigation, she sees a break between the pages, so she grasps the section above the break and peels it back. When she does, she sees a crumpled up page. "Aha..." she says as she unfolds the piece of paper and presses the creases out.

While looking at what was a crumpled piece of paper, she notices right above it what's left of the piece of paper the wind grabbed. She stares at the torn edge of the remaining piece of paper and nods to herself. *Mmm...makes sense the wind couldn't take all of it. No matter what happens, it's now part of me, forever.* She closes up the bound stack of paperwork, puts it back in the case, and closes both suitcase latches. *Kuh click. Kuh click.*

THE OPENING

"Jen?" Jen's mom says from the guestroom doorway.

"Oh, Mom! Sorry...I got lost in thought. I'm so ready for that coffee now!" Jen jumps up from the bed and follows her mother toward the kitchen. The mid-century beige suitcase, with its turquoise embellishments, sits there on the bed, unlocked and unguarded.

As Jen follows her double, she notices that her double's wearing fuzzy black slippers, not shoes. And she notices something else. She's favoring her right foot. With worry in her voice, Jen says, "Mom...why are you limping?"

"Oh...uh...I hurt my foot. Go sit in the dining room with your father. I'm fine."

"Okay," Jen says with a serious tone to her voice as she sits down next to her dad on a bench seat at the dining room table, a table with a weathered barn door table top protected by glass with *Laced* memorabilia inserted between the door and the glass. "Let me get this straight," she says as she places her hands on the table, a table that shows off photos of Jen and Mike taken during the premier at the New York City Royal Nobell Theater on Broadway, a libretto signed by Jen, a playbill signed by the cast and crew, two Broadway tickets and photos of Jen's parents sitting with Jen and Mike in the VIP box. "Dad... you're having chest pain. And Mom, you've hurt your foot." She throws her hands up in the air, shakes her head in disbelief, and blurts out, "Why didn't you tell me this sooner? I could have come earlier!"

"We didn't want to worry you," Maura says as she hands Jen her cup of coffee. "And it's not like I've been having problems with it. It happened today. Do you still take cream in your coffee?"

"I'm betting ya do, babe," her dad says with the nod of his head and a wink.

"Dad's right. I still take cream. So…how did you hurt it? And Mom, sit down for God's sake!"

Jen's mom places the coffee creamer on the table in front of Jen. She then sits down at the table across from Jen and her dad and says, in an upbeat tone, "Well, there's a dead shrub in the backyard, and with the wonderful weather today, I tried to pull it." She pauses for a moment. Then, with a puzzled look she says, "I'm not sure what happened, but when I hit my foot down on the shovel, I felt a burning pain. Now it's all swelled up across the arch. And it feels like I'm walking on a walnut or something."

"Did you make an appointment to get it checked out? Or should we take you to urgent care?" Jen says.

"I don't want to go anywhere. I'll call my podiatrist in the morning."

"All right…sounds like a plan. But…if you need to go to urgent care, let me know. Maybe you should at least ice it. Do you have an icepack? And let's get you over to the recliner so you can elevate it. My God…Mom. This isn't good. You've got to take care of yourself!"

Jen's mom hobbles from the dining room to the living room and sits down on a brown leather recliner. It's an oversized recliner that sits in a living room that looks like it could be on a Western Montana *Better Homes and Gardens* cover spread. With her mom now seated, Jen gently pulls the recliner footrest lever up and asks, "Is this okay?"

"Yes. Thank you, honey."

"Do you want a cup of coffee, Mom?"

"Sure! I'd love one. My cup is next to the coffee pot."

"Okay. I'll be right back."

As Jen makes her way to the kitchen, her dad says, while smiling at her, "Thank God, Jen, you're here to help me with her! She has an icepack in the freezer. Let me get it."

As he walks toward the freezer, Jen stops in her tracks and waves her index finger at him. "And you, Dad. Do you have an appointment? Or do we need to take you to the ER?"

"Nah…I'm good, babe," he says as he opens the freezer door, pulls out an icepack and closes the door. "And besides, we have better things to do and to talk about like how your family is doing."

"We have plenty of time to talk. I'm worried about you, especially with our family history!"

With a serious tone, Jen's dad says, "Your mom and I are just fine. This is life, honey. You can't control it like you can in your writing."

"Dad…You know I know that."

"You're right. I do. What I'm trying to tell ya is…things happen. But there's nothing to worry about. Just relax and enjoy your stay." He holds the icepack out towards Jen. "Here, take this to your mom. While you two catch up, I've got a few projects in the garage I need to finish up."

Jen takes the icy gel pack from his hand. "Thanks, Dad. Let me know if you need any help. And get a glass of water on your way out. With this crazy warm weather, it'll probably be hotter than hell out there."

"Will do," Jen's dad says as he walks away.

Jen walks over to where the coffee pot sits and sets the chilly, flexible icepack on the countertop. She grasps the handle to the glass carafe with her right hand, pulls it away from the warming plate, and then pours the coffee into an earthy brown wheel-thrown coffee mug. As she watches the level of coffee rise in the mug, and listens to the familiar *glug, glug, glug* as she pours the brown brew, she notices a dime-sized hand painted blue barn swallow on the side of the mug. *Oh, Mom…we have so much to talk about.* She stops pouring, returns the carafe to its warming plate, grabs the icepack with one hand, and the cup of coffee with the other and takes both to her mom.

"Thanks, honey," her mom says as she carefully grasps the handle to the hot cup.

After Jen's mom sets the coffee cup on the side table next to her, Jen lifts her mom's injured foot up, carefully pulls the black slipper off her mom's right foot, places the icepack on the footrest and says, "Oh…it's the least I can do." She then sets her mom's foot down on the icepack and asks, "Now, where did I leave my cup?"

"It's over there on the table," Maura says.

"Let me grab it real quick." After getting her cup of coffee, she ambles back toward where her mom is sitting and sits next to her on a matching recliner. "Ahh…this feels nice," Jen says as she lays her head back against the billowy, slick and slippery headrest while carefully balancing her coffee cup in her right hand. While Jen and her mom sit quietly, for a moment, they can hear the clinking sound of glass tumblers touching as Jack—who came back in the house—rifles through the kitchen cabinet where the drinking glasses are stored.

"You've been away for so long, Jen, and we rarely ever hear from you."

"I've had a hard time, Mom, but I've come to grips with what happened, and I'm at a good place now."

"And Mike's okay you came here?"

"Oh, yeah…his only concern was that I drove instead of taking a plane. But I'd rather drive the Jeep than fly," Jen says, grinning at her mom. "Oh! Don't let me forget to tell you about the barn swallow I came across today!"

"Okay, I'll try to remember. How are the kids?"

"Well…Jerry and Amber divorced."

"What?"

"It was a good thing. Once they tied the knot, things seemed to go downhill fast."

"I had no idea, Jen. I'm so sorry to hear that."

"Ever since the divorce, he's submersed himself in work. And he's working in a new field now as a network administrator, and he seems to enjoy it. And Sam, she's an assistant manager at Chipotle and is being trained to take over the restaurant, and Heather...um...I'll talk more about Heather in a bit..."

"Okay. How's little Gabby, honey? It can be hard on little ones when their parent's divorce. I still can't believe she's five now!"

Jen smiles. "Oh, Mom. She's so adorable. And she's doing okay. Jerry is the best daddy, and there's nothing like being a grandma. I love it! When I'm around Gabby, everything's right in the world."

"It sounds like the family is doing so much better. It's been a rough couple of years, Jen. By the way, you said you found a place to put it. What did you mean, sweetie?"

"Remember when Heather was still in intensive care and you and Dad traveled to see her?"

"Uh-huh...I—"

CRASSSH! The horrifying sound of a person falling to the floor mingled with glass shattering and ice cubes hitting the tile floor of the kitchen interrupts the conversation.

"Dad! Oh my God! Mom! Call 911!"

While Jen's mom reaches over and grabs a cellphone from the side table near her chair and dials 911, Jen jumps up from the chair she's sitting on and races to the kitchen. There her dad is, lying on the floor. She kneels down next to him and frantically yells, "Dad! Dad! Can you hear me?"

While she listens for a response from him, she can hear her mom say to the dispatcher, "I think my husband had a heart attack! Please! Please! Send help to 4200 Willow Street! Please!"

Jen, in concert with her mother's final plea with the 911 dispatcher, yells, "Daaad! Please stay with me! DAD!"

UNKNOWING

C upping the end of her cellphone with her palm, trying to keep the sounds of the busy emergency room from infiltrating her conversation, Jen talks to her mom. "He's okay. I know you want to be here. I'll have someone bring you to the hospital tomorrow. They let me talk to him for a minute, and they're moving him to a different room. He said he wants you to rest your foot. And remember, I'm here and can help. The doctor told me he went into cardiac arrest at home. She said it's a miracle he survived! According to her, most people don't survive when their heart stops. We got lucky, Mom! I think the ambulance crew's rapid response helped. Because they got to the house and treated him so fast, it made a difference! In fact, that saved his life! The doctor said he doesn't have any heart damage, but they're keeping him under observation so they can monitor his heart. And he has to have additional tests tomorrow morning—"

"Jen, catch your breath...thank God you were here. He's been having pain lately, but he's so stubborn! He wouldn't listen to me when I told him he needed to see the doctor!"

"Sounds like someone I know. Hmm...and I'm talking to her right now!" Jen says, gently teasing her mom. "I'm going to stay the night at the hospital since I don't have the Jeep. And the ambulance crew, they were wonderful! I still can't believe they let me ride to the ER with Dad."

"Well, you're still well-known out in this neck of the woods. Even though it's been a few years, *Laced* was such a hit, honey. When it first hit Broadway, and folks in our community learned we're your parents, people showed up at the house in droves. And believe it or not, five years later, a few still do. Even our neighbors know we're your parent's. The ambulance crew recognized you, Jen."

"I don't know about that, Mom. I'm just thankful Dad's getting the care he needs. As for you, get some rest tonight. I'll call you in the morning. Oh! And don't forget to call the doctor's office in the morning! You've got to get your foot looked at! We'll figure out how to get you to your appointment."

"I promise I will. I hope you can get some rest. I don't know though…are you sure you don't want to call a taxi and just come home?"

"Nah. I'm fine. A nurse is getting me a recliner and setting it up next to Dad's bed."

"Sounds good, honey. I'll talk to you in the morning. I love you!"

"And I love you! Good night, Mom."

Jen's mom, feeling anxious and worried, hangs up the phone. And then she picks up her slipper, the slipper Jen took off earlier, and carefully places it on her right foot. Then—like an injured seabird—she limps toward the guestroom. When she gets to the guestroom, she flips the light switch on and looks around the vacant room. Thoughts fill her mind. *She was just here, and now she's gone, again.*

As she contemplates Jen's absence, and her husband's heart attack, her dark brown eyes zero in on the unique piece of luggage sitting on the bed. She limps over to the bed and sits down next to the case. She gently wipes her hand back and forth across the worn case as if she were polishing it. *What a remarkable piece of luggage. Huh…it seems familiar.* She then touches the cold chrome suitcase latches with her fingertips. *Jen...where did you put that tragic time in your life? And what is it you want to tell me about Heather?*

Pondering what to do next, she stops polishing the case with her fingers and clasps her hands together in front of her. With her fingers interlocked and resting now on her lap—she sits with eyes aching for answers—staring at the case. And then ... she whispers to herself, "What the hell am I doing?" And before she can think another thought, her fingers separate as she unclasps her hands. And her thumbs find their way to the shiny button locks near the latches. *Kuh click...kuh click.*

With the latches flipped open, she slowly opens the top of the case and stares at its contents, contents no longer shrouded by darkness. *Oh my, Jen...what's this?* she asks herself as she pulls the document Jen's been protecting out of the case. And without further delay, and the document in her hands, she carefully moves her injured body from the edge of the bed to the center of the bed up near the headboard where several fluffy guestroom pillows welcome her. She props her seventy-year-old body up against the pillows all the while looking at what she's holding. The once vacant room, now filled with her presence, listens to the sounds of a mom longing for answers. She takes in a deep breath and then sighs. Feelings of curiosity and guilt escape her lips, "Oh, Jen..."

Meanwhile, Jen now sits on a clinical recliner in a sterile hospital room next to her dad's bedside. And he appears to be resting. As he rests, with eyes closed, Jen mutters under her breath, "Thank God you're okay. But holy shit, Dad!" Over the noise of the blood pressure cuff whirring as it tightens around her dad's arm, she then says, "Dad?"

He faintly whispers, "Yeah, hon?"

"Oh! You can hear me! Are you doing okay?"

"I'm okay...love ya, babe," and he drifts off...

"And I love you...night, Dad."

The sound of the blood pressure cuff deflating slowly evaporates into the cold medicinal air. And Jen pulls her cowboy boots off and curls up in the recliner.

As Jen and her dad close their eyes for the night, Jen's mom, fueled by a spark of optimism, sits at home—alone—with eyes wide open staring at the document within her grip. With no one to hold her back, and deaf to the sudden heavy Oklahoma rain pounding like the hooves of cattle in a cattle stampede on the roof above, she zeroes in on the words in front of her and begins to read...

STAINED GLASS OF <u>US</u>

THE COMPLETE STORY OF THE MUSICAL
STAINED GLASS OF <u>US</u>

by JENNIFER STEIN

PROLOGUE

How is it that a person becomes a statistic? I know how. *My God how I wish I didn't.* I know this girl who became a piece of data. Her name is Heather, and she'll go down in history as a statistic, but she's *so* much more. She's *my* daughter. And this girl—who became a statistic—is also known as the *songbird* in our family. She's a songbird who made her first mark at nine years old on a frigid and windy December night in 1999 at a school Christmas play. And I captured the moment on video, a video I watched earlier today that took me right back to that significant time in Heather's life.

I was sitting next to my husband, Mike, and my eleven-year-old son, Jerry, on *unforgiving*, hard bleacher seats in a packed—and loud—elementary school gymnasium in rural Colorado. My eight-year-old daughter, Sam, who was dressed like an elf, was standing across from us with her classmates on a set of performance bleachers that faced the audience. And the school music teacher, Mr. Jensen, was observing the crowd from an open gymnasium doorway.

I pressed the *Record* button on the camcorder when I saw Mr. Jensen walk up to a microphone on a stand positioned in front of the audience. And I captured him on video saying, "Thank you for coming! The students have been working very hard on learning their parts for the Christmas play, and they hope *you* enjoy the show!" He then picks up the stand with the mic on it and moves it to the side of the bleachers and walks away.

As he disappears into the shadows, a spotlight casts its glow on two students dressed as Mary and Joseph sitting on a bed of straw on the floor between the performance bleachers and the audience—each with a microphone in hand. And even though they're the center of attention, they don't look nervous. Instead, they look calm and collected, and they're looking at Mr. Jensen who now sits at a piano outside the spotlight.

Even though the audience is still noisy, Mr. Jensen nods his head at the student's sitting under the bright light and starts playing the piano. As he moves his fingers from piano key to piano key, I zoom the camera lens in on the student dressed as Mary because the student I'm looking at—the girl in the spotlight—is my daughter, Heather.

Through the viewfinder, I see her. *There she is.* She's sitting on a bed of straw dressed in a homemade baby blue terry-cloth robe with a baby blue headscarf secured to her head with a headband. And she's looking over at the student playing the part of Joseph, and she's smiling. I *love* when she smiles. Oh, my goodness! She's singing now...I can't believe what I hear. Magic is happening right before my very own eyes. She just sang the first four words to the Christmas carol "Joseph Dearest, Joseph Mine." And the only other sound I hear, and that the camcorder mic is also picking up, is the sound of the winter wind howling outside the gym.

I momentarily look away from the viewfinder and look around at the audience. And as I glance to my left and then glance to my right, I'm startled by the sheer number of people staring, with jaws wide open, at Heather's small, round face. Afraid I'll miss something, I look back into the viewfinder and continue to record her singing. And I'm shocked at what's happening. She's hushed—with an angelic voice I've never heard before—the noisy crowd of at least a thousand onlookers. And now...with all eyes on her...she stops singing. The magical moment *seems* to be over...but it's not...the crowd's erupting with a deafening applause…but I'm not clapping. Instead, I'm trying to hold the camcorder steady while recording Joseph's part. And as I'm looking at him through the viewfinder, I'm feeling the weight of someone leaning on me, and I hear the voice of a woman saying, "Wow! Is the girl who just sang your daughter? And has she had singing lessons? That was amazing!"

I wait to respond until Joseph finishes singing his solo, and then—forgetting I'm still recording—I lay the camcorder on my lap and look over at the gal who's waiting for my response. And all that can be seen on the video is the blurry image of my blue jeans, and you can hear me saying, "Oh! Thank you! Yes! She is my girl! And no, she hasn't!"

"Wow!" she says.

"Thank you!" I say while smiling at her. And then I pick up the camcorder from my lap and continue to record the rest of the show.

After the show, parents, teachers and friends caught Heather's dad and me in the hallway, and they all shared how excited they were about Heather's performance. And an overwhelming majority of them mentioned "singing lessons." The truth was—we didn't have money for singing lessons back then. And even though we knew Heather loved to sing, we didn't realize how powerful her vocals were. But her vocal ability *shined* that night, and Mike and I learned she had a *gift*. And from that defining moment on, we nurtured her love of singing.

I remember, on the drive home after the Christmas play, Heather told Mike, Jerry, Sam and me she'd been dreaming of competing on the *North American Stars Competition* show. There she was at nine years old saying, "Guys! I know if Judge Nathan hears me sing, I'll win! I just need him to hear me sing!" All four of us agreed. And to make her dream a reality, she sang every day. She even practiced singing in front of the four of us as if we were the panel of judges on the *North American Stars Competition* show. Months of practicing turned into years, and before Mike and I knew it, Heather was a teenager.

During her teenage years, we encouraged her to make her dream a reality, and we helped her travel—after she auditioned for the *North American Stars Competition* show in New York—to Florida, St. Louis, Tennessee and Texas. However, she never got the chance to sing in front of Judge Nathan. But she *tried* like hell.

Today, Heather no longer sings. It's as if the curtains opened, if only for a while, and Heather was front and center on the stage. For now, the curtains have closed. And we all struggle to grasp what's happening.

While Mike, Jerry and Sam each cope in their own way, I sit alone on a moonless night in my home office—teetering on the edge of sanity—writing about tragedy, my tragedy etched by the breath of Death. This is a far cry from what I've written in the past. I like to write about love and romance. And I still don't know how it happened, but somehow I became known for writing the romantic Broadway hit *Laced*.

As Jen's mom turns the page, she reluctantly stops reading. And her eyebrows wrinkle as she ponders what lies in front of her. *Hmm...what happened here? A page is missing.* Without further thought, she skips forward—past the remnant of what's left of the missing page—and continues to read...

STAINED GLASS

History, with its beginning middle and end, provides me with *unending* intangible tools I can pluck from the invisible space around me and use when I don't know how else to perceive the unthinkable. It's that which has no physical substance that I draw from in order to understand today. And these untouchable tools—as I call them—just might save me as I sync my past with the present so I can move forward.

When I think about Heather—and how she became a number—and why I'm typing these very words, I'm taken back to my beginnings, and in particular, a time when I was ten years old. I'm in an arena in Idaho Falls, Idaho surrounded by statuesque snow-topped mountains, and I'm breathing in fresh mountain air, air that's heavy with the smell of pine trees. I'm wearing a brown cowboy hat, brown cowboy boots, orange plaid pants and a tan long-sleeved shirt, and I have a green kerchief tied around my shirt collar. And I'm showing my one-year-old filly, Penny Candy, at the Idaho Falls City Fair.

I have a firm grasp on Penny Candy's green show lead, and I'm walking her by a panel of judges. As I walk her by the judges, I try to make eye contact with them while I keep Penny Candy's large equine head close to my small bony ten-year-old shoulder on my right side. I can smell her warm sweet horse sweat as she tugs at the lead with her mighty head. And my heart pounds and feels like it's going to jump out of my adolescent chest while her hooves beat the ground and knock up clods of soft dirt as she prances around the showgrounds next to me. Before I know it, Penny Candy and I proudly take third place among the contestants, and I'm handed a milky white silk ribbon.

Somehow, I lost the white ribbon I won that day, but the memory remains. Now, at fifty years old, I stand in the arena of mental illness. This is territory I *never* wanted to be a part of nor dreamed I'd be in. And my heart is pounding as I dare myself to step outside the arena and tell my story. This time though, the trophy isn't a ribbon. Instead, it's the only way I know how to survive after finding Heather at Death's door not long after her bipolar disorder diagnosis.

Heather…Death's door…There she is…There's my girl. Wait! My girl's not right. Something's wrong…She can't hear me. Shit! I slipped back…I don't want to slip back…I can't go back there yet. To get to that *torturous* moment, a moment that has imprisoned my mentality against my will and that tortures my psyche repeatedly by its incessant presence, I had to live. And live I did.

The cowboy theme, that defines my childhood, followed me when in 1983 I moved to Canon City, Colorado. That's where, while working as an editor at a small publishing house, I met my husband Mike, a brown hair, blue eyed Colorado cowboy—also known as my Jon Bon Jovi lookalike—who worked as a guest relations manager at a guest ranch. And that's where our story as a couple begins. Twenty-seven years later, with countless memories captured in photos, and on video, we now have three grown children, one granddaughter, and we live in New York.

As I reflect upon our life, I stare in awe, in my mind's eye, at the beautiful life Mike and I have created. The portrait of us, unlike any family portrait I've ever seen before, is reminiscent of a gorgeous stained glass window. And within the stained glass portrait, we're each made up of different shades of jewel-toned pieces of glass. And other pieces of jewel-toned glass, scattered here and there, create the backdrop which represents moments in our life together as a family. The tin solder that binds the pieces of glass together represents the unbreakable bond we have with one another. And the murky translucence of the glass represents our future. The whole of the stained glass portrait is stunning as each color works in concert with the others. Equally remarkable are the individual pieces that stand out on their own, unique in their shape and color. And embodied within the strong but delicate glass is the fragility of the human condition.

The *stained glass of us* includes many transformations. As I think back, my thoughts turn to 1989. That's when Jerry, my adorable little carbon copy of Mike, was two years old, and Heather, my little round-faced blonde hair and sapphire blue eyed beauty was eight weeks old. During this time, Mike and I took a chance and moved from Canon City, Colorado to Wichita, Kansas after Mike accepted a full-time job as a manager at an exclusive guest ranch in the Wichita area. It was an exciting time in our young married life. We were starting a new life in Kansas which brought us great joy, and we were full of hope for a better future. And the icing on the cake was that, at that time, my mom and dad lived there too. However, our move to Kansas came at a cost—a cost we couldn't foresee.

Not long after our move, our optimistic attitudes came to a *dead* stop. A complete stranger obliterated our hopes and dreams before our very eyes. It was as if he was a monstrous tornado who was hell-bent on chasing us down, chewing us up and spitting us out.

The day that our little family's world changed happened in the summer of 1990, and what occurred was something beyond our comprehension. The *South Central Kansas Signal* worded it like this:

Man arrested in South Central area Monday for breaking, entering and attempted murder. Homeowner grazed by a bullet.

The "homeowner grazed by a bullet" was my husband, Mike. We learned at a later date that the man who shot Mike lives with bipolar disorder, and he had stopped taking his medication. As a result, he became psychotic.

After the shooting, we moved back to Colorado. But eight weeks prior, I gave birth to our third child, Samantha, my little carbon copy of me who we call Sam for short. She was breathtaking and a perfect addition to our growing family. She became the bright sunshiny spot in our lives at a time when we lost hope in ourselves and in mankind. Scarred from the horrific experience, we embraced one another and our three little ones and forged ahead.

Colorado proved to be a great place to raise a family. We ended up settling in Boulder, and over the next nine years we raised our children there. We were fortunate Mike's parents lived only an hour from us in Loveland. Not only did we get to see his parents during the holidays, and on the kid's birthdays, but they provided us with respite as well when we needed to take a break from daily life.

I remember, whenever we needed to take a breather, Mike's dad would drive to Boulder and stay the night with the kids so Mike and I could go to our favorite casino in Cripple Creek, Colorado. The casino was a two hour commute one way, so it helped that we didn't have to worry about driving back to Boulder late at night. Instead, we could focus on playing the slot machines. It was more than that though. We could temporarily get lost mentally in the sights and sounds of the experience.

I can't help but smile when I think back to those trips we made to Cripple Creek. It never failed. Mike and I always arrived late in the afternoon. And every time, as we drove down the street in his 1972 white Chevy four-wheel-drive truck looking for a parking spot, Mike would say, in his best Humphrey Bogart voice, "Jen! I hope you can forgive me!"

And I'd say, in my best Ingrid Bergman voice, "Why? For the love of love, what have you done, Mike?"

And he'd say, "I booked us a hotel room in a ghost town. Don't look. I don't want you to see the abandoned vehicles lining the street." And then we'd burst out laughing, and he'd park the truck. When we'd get out of the truck, we'd hear the sounds of gambling escaping the open casino doors. And the sound of bells ringing as gamblers hit the jackpot, and the sound of coins churning and then dropping into plastic money cups as gamblers collected their winnings sucked us in.

And every time, Mike and I did the same thing. As our ears absorbed the symphony of casino sounds, we'd weave our way in and out of each gaming house while looking for a place to sit. When we found two open slot machines next to each other, in a casino we felt comfortable in, we'd take a seat. Mike would then hand me a twenty-dollar bill, and I'd in turn convert it into nickels using the slot machine I sat at. Like a mirror image, he sat at a gaming machine doing the same.

And before we knew it, the neon metal coin eating machines we sat at, that teased us with play lines and symbols that refused to match, stopped. So we'd enjoy a meal and then settle in for the night at a nearby hotel. Even though we never hit it big on the slot machines, we had a lot of fun trying. It was very refreshing to have time alone and to forget about the worries of parenthood and life.

In time, as the kids got older, they all three attended Bear Creek Elementary School. Eventually, Jerry moved on to Centennial Middle School while the girls completed their elementary school education at Bear Creek. And they all thrived in their school environments. I attribute part of that to the fact that the schools were in a rural like setting away from the hustle and bustle of the bigger cities. And as a bonus, Mike and I grew to know most of the other parents at the kid's schools, and we became close friends with a few.

When Jerry was in sixth grade, we learned that his IQ was higher than average. Based on this discovery, and per his teacher's recommendation, we transferred him to a gifted and talented class where he enjoyed a more challenging curriculum. Besides excelling academically, he was also a very inquisitive and playful child. But what stands out to me was how calm and content he was as a child. These qualities, about his personality, proved to be helpful years later with Heather.

Heather relished in her popularity at the school, and she too, like her big brother, was inquisitive and playful as a child. However, she expressed an independent streak that concerned us, and it was a streak that would often get her into trouble. Despite her troublesome behavior, her music teacher supported her love of singing, encouraged her to write lyrics, and gave her several solo parts in school concerts. But it was like there were little red flags popping up such as her need for attention and difficult behavior most mornings while getting ready for school, to name a few.

Sam also relished in her popularity at school, and she presented early in life with an independent attitude like Jerry and Heather. But her independent nature was more constructive. For example, when she was in second grade, her teacher would ask her during group time to supervise the class while she worked with a small group of students in another area of the classroom. Sam loved that. To this day, she still likes to tell this story. She was also curious and playful. And like her brother, she was an even-tempered and happy child which came in handy later on with Heather.

It was great that the teachers at Bear Creek and Centennial Middle recognized our kid's strengths. That was important to Mike and me, and we appreciated it. We felt confident that our kids were getting a high quality education.

During our years in Boulder, Mike worked as a guest ranch manger in the area. Besides managing the ranch, he worked part-time at Creak Hospital as an EMT. And he was also an active volunteer firefighter with the local fire department.

While Mike worked outside of the house, I stayed home and took care of the kids. The decision that I'd become a stay-at-home mom was a decision Mike and I made when we started our family. It made sense. As an editor, I could do freelance work from home.

As I tended to our children, and freelanced, I discovered an untapped passion. I found that I enjoy writing. And the genre that interested me back then was romance. So while Jerry was in middle school and the girls were in elementary school, I wrote *Laced*, my first romance novel.

Within a short time of writing *Laced*, and sending off query letters, a premier romance book publishing company offered me a publishing contract. And when *Laced* made it to the bookstore shelves, I experienced a great deal of success—right away. To this day, I still can't believe how fast it all happened. And then, at the blink of an eye, while on a book signing tour, I met playwright Gene Oliver and was thrust into the world of Broadway; a world which was uncharted territory for me at that time. It was only after he doggedly pursued me that I took his advice and created the musical version of *Laced*. As a result, I assembled a creative team to assist me in the making of the musical. There was a catch though. The team members that Gene recommended I hire were all based out of New York.

Out of a need to work closely with the musical creative team I assembled, and with money no longer an issue, Mike and I moved our family to New York. This meant we would have to move our family across the country far from anything we'd ever known. With that, a new beginning started for all five of us. And it would be a year we'd never forget.

It was the year 2001, and it was August. And for the first time in our lives we got to experience what it's like to have the help of a moving company, and we took full advantage of it by jump starting our move. Instead of focusing on packing, we focused on getting to New York as soon as we could.

Since I was due to meet with the musical score creator in mid-August, and we wanted the kids to start school at the beginning of the new school year, we made the move around the first of August. And we didn't mess around. We packed up the kids and our beautiful family dog, a golden retriever we named Clinker, and we drove east.

I remember feeling excited about the move. And yet, the day we drove away from our home in Colorado and headed east, I was a saddened passenger who felt unsettled about leaving behind the Northwest and our family and friends. Regardless, we moved forward with our plans and made the trek east.

While on the road, Gene called and told us to check out Laurel Hollow. He said it was a great place to raise a family. So we took his advice and toured the village as soon as we got to New York. And we liked it, so that's where we initially moved. But because we were so excited to make the move, and had left Colorado without a new home to go to, we ended up temporarily living in a hotel. While living at the hotel, Jerry began his freshman year of high school. Heather started sixth grade, and Sam started fifth grade.

Within a few weeks' time, we moved into a rental house. Even though we didn't feel settled yet, we got busy. Mike looked for work, the kids began their adjustment to a new school system, and I promptly started working with the *Laced* team.

Then, on the eleventh of September, I received a phone call I'll never forget. My mother-in-law called me. And from the way she talked, I was afraid there was an intruder in her house at that moment. She screamed into the phone, "Oh, my God! We've been attacked!" She choked on her words asking,

"Where are you? Mike? The kids?" Before I could answer, she asked, "Are you watching the news?"

I anxiously replied, "No! We're all home sick with a stomach bug, Mom." As our conversation unfolded, I ran to the television set and turned it on. From then on, the TV was on for days while we watched in horror the devastation that occurred at the World Trade Center. It terrified us, and we were afraid to leave the house. Little did I know that the evil cloud of fury—that befell the World Trade Center—was an ominous sign of something dark coming our way as well.

Despite the challenges, we didn't slow down. Instead, Mike and I decided, after renting for a year, that we were ready to buy a house. We were ready for a home of our own. And as a result, we found a nice property in Kensington, New York. And finally, everything was in place—or so it seemed. Once again, we lived in our own place. And Mike changed career paths and pursued a degree in information technology. I took a temporary break from the development of the musical and enrolled the kids in the Kensington school district. And I'd like to say, on that note, everything went smoothly from there; Mike and I raised the kids and are now enjoying an empty nest. But fate wouldn't have it that way.

THE PULL BACK

S o here I am, *a mom*, not just a Broadway writer, but a *mom* numb from the horrific experience of finding my daughter in the state I found her, numb from the realization that someone I love lives with a mental health disorder, numb from the challenges myself and my family have faced so far regarding the mood disorder she lives with, and numb with fear of what's coming. And I'm twisting, drawing, pulling and playing with words trying to feel.

And as I take hold of words and grasp onto them with all my might, as if they're a lifeline pulling me, word by word, back from the black hole of psychological shock I've fallen into, I'd like to take you on a journey for a moment. Imagine, if you will, that you're attending an opera for the first time, and not just any opera but a *tragic* opera. For many, it would be a once-in-a-lifetime event.

Regardless, here you are. And you're standing outside an opera house, an opera house only you can imagine. As you stare at the building, you hear people talking. Their voices are coming from behind you. In response, you turn to see who they are. As you look back, you notice you're first in line to enter the theater. And then you turn to look at the building again. As you refocus on the opera house, a set of gigantic dark brown wooden doors open, and you walk inside. As you enter the building, you see in the distance another set of doors. This time though the doors look like they're made of gold. And they pull you in.

As you continue to walk toward the closed, gilded doors you notice a doorman standing to the right of the doors. He's dressed in a gray suit and a matching top hat. As you approach him, he greets you with a quick nod of his head, and he holds out a white-gloved hand. In response, you give him your ticket. As the ticket rests into place on the palm of his hand, the doors automatically swing open.

You stride forward and step foot inside the auditorium, an auditorium that appears dark. As your eyes adjust to the darkness, a female usher, with a black and white pinstriped vest and matching pants, greets you and motions for you to follow her. And so you do. You quietly walk behind her as she escorts you to the front-row. As you follow close behind, what seemed to be a dark auditorium comes alive as you notice flickering lights coming from candle sconces that line the wall you're walking next to. Before you know it, you've reached the front-row and the usher motions for you to sit down on a vacant seat in the middle of the row next to two strangers. As you sit down, she disappears.

You look at the vacant stage in front of you. And then you look around the dimly lit auditorium. At first, you see people filtering in and filling the vacant seats behind you. And then you notice in all its beautiful glory, the interior of the theater, a theater ornately decorated with elegant cranberry red velvet upholstered seating, towering balconies painted in gold, and crystal chandeliers dripping from the elaborate ceiling above. You then turn to face the empty, grandiose, weathered and worn old oak stage, a stage with a massive scarlet red crushed velvet grand drape hanging in the background.

As your mind absorbs where you're at, the cool temperature of the opera house, and the smell of sweet old oak, take over your senses and envelope you. And you relax into this magnificent space. And you ready yourself for what's coming.

Now, as you wait for the show to begin, I invite you to think about parenthood. Regardless if you are a parent or not, do you see a similarity between the theater seating, the stage or any other feature in the theater and parenting? One similarity I see is that parents have an incredible firsthand view of their children's lives. Parents are like audience members with front-row seats. And who wouldn't want a front-row seat? I know Mike and I want to be at the forefront of our children's lives no matter how old they become. And watching each one of them grow into the people they've become today has been wondrous. And what an accomplishment! We did our part. We raised them. And now we get to sit back and enjoy the fruits of our labor.

But wait…just as Mike and I sit back and take it all in, reality creeps up on me, and I remember, I'm watching a tragedy unfold. The tragedy isn't someone else's. And the show you're ready to watch doesn't belong to anyone but me and Mike. We're the two strangers sitting next to you. And it's our tragedy. I don't want this front-row seat now. This isn't what I envisioned. I feel powerless…and I feel utter despair. How can I stop this? Like a dangerous rockslide roaring down a mountain, I can't…and the grand drape opens.

And there it is—the beautiful *stained glass of us*—lying haphazardly on the old opera floor. My songbird stands on the stage with her voice silenced. She's frozen in time—with Death ready to take his next victim—lingering in the air around her. My son turns away and steps off the stage because the pain is almost too great for him to bear. My youngest and ever so innocent daughter responds with surprising anger. She snaps at her sister and then recoils into the depths of sadness. My husband, ever so optimistic and strong, responds by touching my frozen songbird's icy face with his warm hands, and then he drops to his knees and sobs at her feet. And I…dazed and full of sadness, with eyes blurry from crying, slowly reach down and pick up the *stained glass of us*. I then gently dust it off and begin to timidly sing and dance since the show goes on no matter how hard I internally scream.

THE CODE

I open my eyes and see nothing but a blurry image. In response, I close my eyes again and re-open them. The image is still blurry. But now I see the outline of a person. And I can see that we're separated by a dark table, a table so dark it disappears into nothingness. And sitting on the table is a large crystal ball. I try to focus on the facial features of the crystal ball gazer sitting in front of me, but I close my eyes yet again because the magical glowing sphere is so bright. When I re-open my eyes this time, I still can't make out the facial features of the crystal ball gazer, but I'm able to see the figure's hands move over and hover above the ball of light.

In a monotone voice, the figure teasing me with its presence says, "Jen, I see that you'll marry." The figure's breath—heavy with truth—pulls me in closer. And then, I hear, "Light will be with you. And then...darkness comes. Someone who lives with bipolar disorder will gravely harm your husband."

In an incredulous tone I counter, "You're crazy!"

The figure doesn't respond. Then I hear, "One of your future children will develop bipolar disorder as well and will suffer horrifically."

Horrified by what I hear, I shout, "You're mad as a fucking hatter!"

Again, the figure doesn't react. Instead, the figure says, "The code to the bipolar pendulum..." And then—the voice fades away. I strain to hear what I'm being told...my ears feel like they're bleeding as I strain to hear more of this voice...

I beg and plead with that which I can't see, "Please! Tell me more!" Before I can breathe another breath, I wake up trembling. And I realize the fortune teller was right, and I'm the one who's wrong. And all I'm left with is guilt racing through my veins.

As my brain wakes up, the guilt eases. But my mind takes over where guilt left off. And I realize how real the nightmare was. Questions swirl around in my mind. *My girl, she was diagnosed with late adolescent bipolar disorder. But how did this happen? Did manic depression cross an invisible plane through the shooter in Kansas and gain entrance to our lives through Heather?* I physically shake off the last thought and dismiss it—because I've had it often—and I tell myself, *Wake up, Jen.* And so I do.

But as I lay here and look up at the ceiling, I remind myself that Mike, Jerry, Sam and I don't live with bipolar disorder. And, according to my mom and my mother-in-law, no one in the family on either side lives with it, including past generations. So then where the hell did it come from? God damn it! I have to figure it out so I can unlock the code to the bipolar pendulum and rescue my girl from her illness. Perhaps the code I seek is right in front of me. Maybe it's hiding within the bizarre guilt I feel, guilt I've had ever since starting a family.

I can trace the sickening feeling of guilt first washing over me when I learned I was pregnant with Jerry. It happened after I drank a beer with some friends. When I drank the amber brew, I didn't know I was pregnant so I didn't give it a thought. But when I learned I was pregnant, a few weeks later, I worried that the beer I drank had to have harmed my unborn baby.

But I worried for no reason. In June of 1987, I gave birth to a healthy baby boy. Two years later, in October of 1989, I gave birth to Heather, and like a game of dominoes, two years later, in March of 1991, I gave birth to Samantha. All three pregnancies were normal. And Mike and I were parents to three—healthy—beautiful children.

Regardless, the *mommy guilt*—as I call it—took hold of me early on, and it became rampant when Heather was diagnosed with mental illness in her late teens. And it has a hold of me at this moment and is weighing me down. It's pressing my body, through the dense memory foam mattress I'm lying on, into the hardwood floor below. Before I fully suffocate, I remember what I did the day Heather told me about her diagnosis.

I sat down at my computer and typed. It was the only way I could cope with the guilt. I picked through my memories like a paleontologist digging and picking through ancient soil hoping to uncover a part, if not all, of what caused the mood disorder of my daughter. And as I typed, mental snapshots of Heather flooded my mind.

And then I landed on a significant memory, a memory ripe with possibility. This memory of all memories comes from the day I delivered Heather. There I am. I'm in the delivery room. And the doctor has induced labor. I've opted to have an epidural because I didn't have pain medication when I had Jerry, and I don't want to relive the pain I had while delivering my first born.

Since epidural anesthesia is a new experience for me, I'm nervous. I don't like needles, but with each wave of contractions, I'm outwardly begging for any pain relief I can get. As I beg, Mike rubs my back, and then he says, "The anesthesiologist is here, Jen!"

I don't answer him because I'm waiting for the mother of all contractions to abate. When the contraction lessens to the point I can talk, I blurt out, "Thank God!" And then I close my eyes. I can hear Mike saying, "Breathe, Jen…Jen…don't forget to breathe. Inhale through your nose…hold it. Exhale—"

"Exhale! You have no fucking clue how much this hurts!" And then I hear someone other than Mike talking, and I open my eyes.

It's the anesthesiologist, and he's saying, "I need you to lie on your left side."

"Okay," I say while nodding at him and rolling my heavy baby laden body to the left. I'm speechless again, but my brain's alive with thought after thought. *The nurse is now adjusting my gown, and she's moving it to the side. I can feel the touch of cold air on the skin of my back...My back is bare...There's nothing protecting my skin...I feel so vulnerable.*

I'm feeling something wet and cold. And the anesthesiologist is saying, "You're feeling the cleansing solution...I have to apply it first."

I blurt out, "Oh! It's so cold!" *I'm feeling a sensation, like a sting...oh no! I think I'm gunna puke. I'm feeling so much pressure...okay...I'm all right...I think the catheter's in.*

And then, what happened next was one of the most bizarre things I've ever experienced. My entire pregnant body levitated and then dropped onto the delivery bed as if the anesthesiologist electrocuted me. And the room fell silent.

There I was lying on the delivery bed scared. And it seemed to take forever for anyone to respond. I felt all alone with only my thoughts to keep me company. *Hello? Has time stopped? What's happening? I think I'm in shock...I can't talk...Why's the room getting dark? I hear something... someone.*

"Jen? Are you okay? I haven't finished yet...we're almost done...hang in there."

In pain and shaken by what happened, I nervously reply, "I'm okay." After a few minutes, the anesthesiologist quietly, and carefully, completes the procedure. Finally, I'm pain free.

Since I was in active labor, the strangeness of that event didn't linger long because Mike and I were busy having a baby. And at 10:59 p.m. on a warm October night, I gave birth to our first girl. She weighed seven pounds thirteen ounces, and she was a beautiful sight to behold.

No matter what happened, Heather was as healthy as could be, and I recovered without any problems. But wait. What if?

I know that there's no correlation. However, it strikes me as an unusual event. While I was in active labor, it felt like the anesthesiologist electrocuted me. I know this sounds far-fetched, but what if Heather was harmed during the event? And what if that's the cause of her mood disorder? When I find myself ruminating about this experience, I express my proposed theory to Mike. And he acknowledges what happened and then simply puts an end to the musing like a candle snuffer extinguishes a burning candle.

The only other memory I've brought to light that could have something to do with Heather's illness is from Heather's teen years. And it involves drugs. Like many teens do, Heather experimented with drugs, but she also self-medicated. And she was self-medicating during the time she was officially diagnosed. Therefore, it's plausible to me that the self-medicating Heather did caused enough of a mood swing that when she sought counseling, the counselor was convinced that Heather had bipolar disorder. But perhaps Heather was high. Or maybe she was depressed after not drinking for a few days. Alcohol is a depressant, so maybe it appeared that she had a diagnosable mental illness when in fact she was coming off of a mind-altering substance.

This may or may not be plausible, but I've always felt guilty about not being with her when the counselor diagnosed her. In my mind, I like to think, if I was there, I could have shared my concerns with her counselor and said, "Hey! Wait a minute! STOP! She's high! How can you screen her for a mental illness? She smoked pot right before coming in here! Let's address this when she's not self-medicated!"

The realist in me tells me I'll never know what *caused* Heather's illness. I've come to learn that it's a biological condition. However, my brain doesn't want to believe that. Like a paleontologist—I keep digging—and the fortune teller keeps knocking…

POPPY

I'm sitting at my desk in my office after dragging myself out of bed. And I don't how, but I made a pot of coffee. The cold, empty coffee cup in my hand is proof. And I want a refill, but a black-and-white picture, sitting on my desk, of a bouquet of Oriental poppies has captured my attention. It's a picture Heather took, during the workshop stage of *Laced*, at a studio in Upper Manhattan. And even though the colors of the flowers are missing in the photo, I remember the neon tangerine-orange colored poppies as if I were back in the studio the day she took it. And the more I look at the photo, the more I realize Heather's like an Oriental poppy in a field of daisies. And it started in utero.

I've given birth three times, and naturally, each pregnancy was different. But it was when I carried Heather that I experienced something unusual. During my second trimester, her fetal movements were volatile. One moment...she was still...and the next...she'd kick me hard. Her movements were so forceful that whenever Mike laid his hand on my pregnant belly, he'd tease me and say, "Whoa, Jen! I'm telling you! We're having twin boys!"

And I'd say, "Oh, stop it, Mike."

He'd reply, "I'm serious! And they're going to be football players when they grow up!" As my pregnancy with her wore on, I started to believe him as I watched my belly move and contort in ways I'd never seen before, and felt kicks that only a future *skilled* football player could do. Then, to our surprise, I gave birth to one *darling* little girl.

And our *darling* little girl grew fast, as all kids do, and surprised us yet again on her third birthday. Her birthday present was a sixteen inch kid's bike. When she saw her new wheels, she screamed excitedly and said, "A bike!" She then giggled, mounted the bike for the first time, and—without training wheels—rode off. There she was at three years old riding a bike. She had just accomplished the ability to recite her ABC's and count to ten—and I was watching her ride down the street on a bike, without help.

My dad happened to be in town visiting, and he witnessed the event. And his reaction was comical. As Heather rode away from us, his relaxed stance changed to a military stance—and he's never been in this military. As he stood at attention, he proudly gushed, "Now that's unusual!" Mike and I agreed. And we knew it was extraordinary. We called extended family and shared the news, as we usually did regarding any new milestones with Jerry, Heather and Sam, and then we carried on with our busy life.

It wasn't until about four years later, when Heather was around the age of seven, that I noticed—once again—something different. I had decided to re-teach myself how to crochet a granny square. And I was playing around with a gold-colored crochet hook and a magenta-colored skein of yarn. While I worked at forming a slipknot around the hook, the girls walked up and watched what I was doing. And then, they both plopped down beside me on the couch. With great interest, Heather said, "Mom? How are you doing that?"

Sam chimed in and said, "Yeah, Mom! What are you doing?"

I said, "I'm re-teaching myself how to crochet a granny square. Do you want to learn?"

In unison, they giggled and said, "Yes! I want too!"

I was thrilled they wanted to learn how to crochet, so I gave Sam a crochet hook and a small blue ball of yarn, and I gave Heather a crochet hook and a small white ball of yarn. And then, I showed them how to make a slip knot, a chain stitch, a single crochet stitch and a double crochet stitch. And in that one sitting, Sam managed to crochet a small, loose and lopsided blue granny square. Before I could say, "Great job, Sam!" she threw the granny square on the couch next to me and ran outside to play. I couldn't help but smile as I looked at her lopsided granny square and heard the door close behind her. I was *so* proud of her.

While Sam played outside, Heather continued to crochet, and I did the same. When Heather finished crocheting her motif, she said, "Mom! Look!"

I looked up from the piece I was crocheting, and I couldn't believe my eyes. Heather had crocheted a perfectly square white granny square. Her tension was spot on—and to be honest— her granny square looked better than the one I was trying to finish. I excitedly replied, "Heather! That's amazing! I'm *so* proud of you!"

She smiled back at me and then said, "Mom? Do you have more yarn?" And from that moment on, Heather crocheted every chance she could get. And she went above and beyond crocheting granny squares. She crocheted purses, blankets and clothes. And she didn't just crochet granny square style. Instead, she developed her own style of crocheting—my Oriental poppy in a field of daises.

SOS

I stood at the kitchen window, after I refilled my coffee cup, and watched a boy on a bike ride by the house. As he zipped by, the red safety flag attached to the back of his bike caught my attention as it whipped around in the wind. While I watched the red pennant shaped inanimate object move about, it reminded me that Mike and I concluded—after I found Heather—that there were little red flags, like her attention-seeking behavior, that faintly waved throughout her childhood. And though we were being warned, we didn't seek help. Heather...Death's door...there she is. I'm slipping back again. Damn it!

I turn away from the memory of Heather in the state I found her, as if I'm turning away from a mirror in a house of mirrors, and I look at her little round four-year-old face. As I look into her sapphire blue eyes, while I push the paperwork from an editing project I'm working on to the side, she says, "Mommy...I can't walk. It hurts." In this moment, her childhood owies and boo-boos have given way to a full on medical concern.

Frightened by her announcement, Mike and I take her to our pediatrician for an evaluation. In the exam room, he asks her to describe her symptoms, and then he asks her to join him out in the hallway. She does as he asks and follows him out the door. And Mike and I follow close behind. He then directs her to walk to the other end of the hallway, and she does—but she limps as she walks away from us. He then says, "Okay. You can stop now, Heather." While he continues to assess her, diseases such as muscular dystrophy and cerebral palsy are racing through my mind.

Minutes later, he says, "I'm not sure what's going on Mr. and Mrs. Stein. I'd like to ask you to make another appointment. Keep a record of any new symptoms and complaints and bring it with you to the next appointment." Mike and I agree and take Heather home.

Later that day, while running cold water over strained spaghetti noodles, I overhear Mike talking in another room. But I can't make out what he's saying. And I'm not concerned, until I hear him say, over the sound of water running from the faucet, "Heather! I can't believe you'd do that!" I turn the faucet off, set the noodles down and head to the living room. And when I get there, Mike looks at me and says, "She just *walked* by me. She didn't limp. She walked."

"What?" I say.

"When she saw me look at her, she limped again, Jen!"

A sense of relief washes over me because I know she's okay. And then reality sets in. She was faking it. She's not in pain. She can walk just fine. Baffled that she faked an illness, we scold her for her behavior and cancel the follow-up appointment.

I turn away from the memory of the *fake* leg pain, as if I'm still in a house of mirrors, and I'm holding a phone in my hand. I'm talking with the school nurse at Bear Creek Elementary School. Heather, who's now in first grade, is in her office. The nurse is saying, "Mrs. Stein, Heather has become a regular fixture here in my office."

"A regular fixture?"

"Yes. She's not causing any harm, but I thought I should let you know. She comes to my office *daily*."

"Daily?"

"Uh-huh…complaining that *something* hurts. It just seems a bit unusual."

"I'm so sorry! I'll talk to her about it!"

And I do, and it seems to help. But then—she gets seriously hurt. As if I'm still in a house of mirrors, I turn to yet another memory and see her nine-year-old face. And she's running up to me—bleeding—with a bite mark on her finger and Sam in tow.

"What happened, Heather?" I say.

Sam says, "She put a cat in the ice-cream bucket you told her to throw away."

"A cat?"

"Yeah, Mom," Jerry says. "And when Clinker saw it, the cat clawed her, jumped out of the bucket and ran away."

I whisk her off to the bathroom, clean her wound, bandage it and then talk to the kids about the importance of not picking up stray animals. I then tell Mike what happened when he gets home from work. And I don't give it another thought—until morning.

I'm waking Heather up for school, and I'm seeing strange marks on her arm. They look like red streaks of chalk, and they're originating from the cat scratch. And they're angry looking. I yell, "Mike! Come here! I'm in Heather's room!"

Alarmed, Heather sits up, looks at her arm and says, "What's that?"

"Don't worry, honey. Dad will be right here," I say.

He runs into her room, kneels down next to her bed, examines her arm and then says, "Don't mess around! Get her to the doctor—now!"

I don't hesitate. I take her, as fast as I can, to see the pediatrician. And it turns into a horrific experience for Heather. The doctor orders two shots of penicillin—immediately. And he wants them injected into her thighs. Before Heather and I can react, a nurse walks into the exam room with two syringes in her hand. Heather yells at her, "No! I don't want shots!"

The nurse replies, "You'll be fine, dear. It's a good thing you have shorts on. We won't need you to change into a gown. Mom, please hold her hands down." I look at the nurse like she's crazy, so she calls for help. And before I know it, an assistant runs into the room, holds Heather's hands down, and the nurse administers the shots. I'm sick to my stomach. I didn't protect my girl.

Before I know it, she's discharged from the clinic. And she's as white as a ghost. As we walk out the door, I grasp her arm. But she pulls away from me and says, "Stop! Don't touch me." I nod at her to let her know I got the message, and we continue to walk toward our car.

As we walk across the parking lot, a woman drives by us with her car window down. And she's glaring at me. I feel the "I'm to blame" poisonous *mommy guilt* emotion, like hot mercury in a fever thermometer, rise. Then, as I help Heather get into the car, I hear someone from across the parking lot yell, "What's wrong with you?" I turn to see who it is and see it's the same lady who glared at me as she drove by. I turn away from her and focus on Heather. And then I hear, "Why didn't you carry her? Or at the very least, why didn't you get the car while she waited for you?! You're a terrible mom!" I act like I don't hear her, and instead, I get Heather home as fast as I can.

I'm biting my fingernails on the drive home because the doctor told me, "You need to find and *trap* the cat so Animal Control can test it for rabies. We'll call Animal Control for you. But listen, if you don't find the cat, Mrs. Stein, you'll have a difficult decision to make. Without a cat, Heather will need to start the rabies vaccine series—immediately. I'm sorry. Time's not on your side. If you can't prove the cat doesn't have rabies, you'll be taking a gamble with Heather's life if you don't get her vaccinated. If you wait for to her to have symptoms—it could be too late."

To my relief, Animal Control doesn't mess around when they get the call, and they're at the house when I pull into the driveway. And they've already set the trap for the feral cat. While I'm helping Heather get out of the car, one of the officer's approaches me and says, "There's nothing for you to do. Just give us a call if the cat shows up. We'll take it from there." I tell the officer I understand, and from that moment on, the entire family watches for any sign of the cat.

Nighttime comes and goes, and before we know it, all five of us are scrambling to get to the trap. And when we run up to it—we see that it's empty. Without hesitation, we rush Heather to the hospital, and she receives the first of eight shots that day in her upper arm. Even though the shots are spaced out over the next four weeks, Heather finds each injection she receives to be excruciating. Even so, Mike and I are confident we made the right decision. With our girl's life on the line, there would be no risk taking. This was no cry for attention. Gone from my mind, like blackboard dry erase markings wiped clean, were her past attempts to garner our attention. Instead, Mike and I focused on the crisis at hand and continued to move forward as we had the demands of three rapidly growing children to meet.

BLIND

The more I write, the closer I get to writing about the moments that led up to my mental fall into an abyss of mental shock. I go to bed after writing and wonder if I'm the one now with a mental illness. As Heather appears to be more stable, at this moment, I question my stability. Maybe there isn't a story to tell. Maybe I'm expressing a narcissistic part of my personality thinking my own writing can save me—like I'm my own heroine. But I've saved the characters I created for other works. Why the hell then can't I save myself?

Whether or not I can save myself, I feel alone as I write. And then, I remember why I'm here. I pick myself up, the lone ballet dancer I am in the *Opera Show of Us*. And I continue to timidly sing. Despite how lonely I feel, I push on. My toes are barely touching the old, worn oak stage. They're dragging gently along. The silk ballet slippers I wear are becoming tattered and worn as I lift up my family, as well as myself, and carry the *stained glass of us* along.

I'm struggling to write at this point because as Heather grew older, life grew more difficult for her, and for those who love her. So once again, I play with the words I type because then I can avoid conjuring up the tangled mess of some very sad memories. And when I revisit old memories, the "I'm to blame" poisonous emotion in the *mommy guilt* thermometer rises. I thought I had dealt with the guilt. I know I'm not responsible for a biological condition, and yet I still feel an intimate and deep connection to Heather's mental illness because ultimately and unarguably, I gave birth to her. Any pain and distress she experiences I feel responsible for because— I'm mom.

When Mike and I moved our family to New York, Heather started to exhibit *normal* teen rebellion, so we thought. After all, she was only twelve years old when we made the move to the Big Apple. And it occurred while we were temporarily living in Laurel Hollow.

It started with a dance, a dance she wasn't allowed to attend. And it has an air of innocence to it. I don't think Heather meant to be unruly. I think Heather was being Heather. And I wonder if in her mind she imagined she was a princess going to a ball.

The ball wasn't a formal dance. Instead, it was a fall dance on a Saturday night. And it was a dance Mike and I knew nothing about until Heather approached us about it, a week beforehand. When she asked us if she could go, we told her she wouldn't be able to because my mom, who lived out of state, had made plans to visit us well before we knew about the dance. And Mike and I had pre-planned a sight-seeing adventure for the kids and my mom in upstate New York. It was a getaway we were *really* looking forward to. And to be honest, I think I was looking more forward to it than Mike or my mom because I had been working day in and day out those first few months on the musical and needed a few days off. I felt bad for Heather, but I didn't give it another thought. There were times we couldn't do *all* the things the kids wanted to do, especially last minute.

The same evening we told Heather she wouldn't be able to go to the dance, she asked if she could stay the night with a new friend. We were glad to hear she was making new friends. So we agreed that she could stay the night, and we took her to her friend's house.

Lo-and-behold, when Mike and I picked her up the following day, she sauntered out to the car carrying a lavender floor-length gown in her arms. As she slid into the backseat of the car, she carefully positioned the borrowed gown on her lap, a gown protected by a clear plastic garment bag. The sight of the gown puzzled us, so we both took turns questioning her about it. She told us her friend was lending it to her for the dance. She had totally disregarded what we told her the evening before. Mike and I told her to return the dress immediately, but she resisted and argued back. She spun the conversation around to the point we questioned our own initial intentions. And due to the frigid cold that day, instead of continuing to argue with her, we whisked her home. Once home, we all agreed she'd return the dress. The conversation ended with her stating she'd make arrangements to give the dress back to her newfound friend.

The following week flew by. Before I knew it, the weekend arrived, and it was time to pick mom up from the airport. The plan was that I'd pick her up and take her to our house for part of the day, and then we'd all head upstate.

The day's events went according to plan until my mom and I were back at the house. We were standing in the kitchen talking, and enjoying a cup of coffee, while Mike packed the car. As Mom and I busily chattered, Heather walked into the kitchen. But I almost didn't recognize her. Instead of seeing my girl who always wore blue jeans and a t-shirt, I saw a princess.

There she was wearing the borrowed lavender gown. With her cute, bouncy, chin length hair framing her round smiling flawless tween face, she asked, "Mom, will you take me to the dance?" I didn't immediately respond. I was speechless. I glanced at my mom with eyes begging for help. Mom, an innocent bystander, looked at me in bewilderment. My poor mother, she didn't know what was happening.

I felt my blood pressure rise, and I said, "I have a problem with this young lady!" I remember thinking I must have looked like an incompetent parent. Regardless, I told Heather, "Stay here with your Grandma! I'll be right back!" I then stormed out of the kitchen.

I found Mike and Jerry out in the driveway loading everyone's suitcases into the trunk of the car. I pulled Mike to the side. We had a brief discussion about what Heather had done and decided, rather than cause more upset, we'd change our plans and take mom upstate the next day. And with that, Mike and I drove Heather to the school dance. Interestingly enough, incidents like this never happened with Jerry or Sam. Heather *clearly* marched to a different drummer.

That was the beginning of the rebellion that seemed to walk next to Heather as if it were a close friend. Another incident that stands out in Heather's young life happened on a Friday night. Heather wanted to have a girls' night at the house so with our approval she invited a few girlfriends over. Before we knew it, the night turned into a disaster.

Mike and I were unaware that the girls had locked themselves in their room. During this time, Mike was downstairs in the living room watching TV, and I was in our home office, also downstairs. I was on a conference call with Roland, co-producer and director of *Laced*—a genuine teddy bear at heart disguised as a consummate professional—who likes to work twenty-four seven.

And at some point that evening, I heard a commotion outside. I told Roland I needed to go and would call him right back. I then got up from my desk, went to the living room where Mike was sitting and asked him, "Do you hear something going on outside?"

He said, "Yeah...what the hell's going on out there?" He jumped up from his recliner, whipped the drapes back, looked out the window and said, "You've gotta be kidding me?

What the hell? There's a bunch of boys out there in the front yard looking up at the girl's window! Are you serious? They're throwing something!" And before he said another word, he bolted outside, and as he did, I heard him shout, "What's going on out here?" At that point, all I could hear was someone's muffled response. I couldn't make out what was being said, but in return Mike said, "You better get the hell out of here or I'm calling the cops!"

When Mike came back inside, I didn't bother to ask him what all the commotion was about. Instead, I went directly upstairs to find out what was going on with the girls. But I ran into a locked door. I had to knock several times before they relented and unlocked it. As I opened the door, Sam squeezed by me, with her head down, and walked out of the room. When I asked her what had happened, she whispered, without looking up, "Heather and her friends were lifting their shirts up for the boys."

Stunned by what she told me, I said, "Go downstairs—now! I need to talk to Heather." After she walked away, I walked into the bedroom, and I didn't mince words. I told Heather's friends, "You need to call your parent's. It's time to go home." That was a difficult moment. What a mess. I hated to tell her friends they had to leave, but I was beyond disappointed with their behavior and Heather's. I walked her friends downstairs, and to the front door, and once they left, I headed back up to Heather's room.

I sat down on the edge of her bed and talked to her about the incident. She didn't seem phased by it. She replied, "Mom, Beth's mom is a stripper."

I was mad, sad and confused in that moment. And I didn't mean to, but I blurted out, "Oh, my God! A stripper? What?! Why are we talking about stripping now?" And then I shut my mouth. I didn't know what to say next. And I didn't want Heather to misunderstand me. I knew I needed to be sensitive to what occurred, but it wasn't easy. Somehow, we got through it though.

Also, on that same night, I found out Heather and her girlfriends had made plans to run away. It seemed the problems that night were escalating rather than subsiding. And each time the issue at hand was more serious than the last. It was like Heather's behavior was a musical note increasing towards a crescendo building higher and higher. Still, Mike and I continued to believe we were dealing with adolescent rebellion.

We also increased our parental stance. We drew the line so to speak. We came down harder on Heather each time she misbehaved. And before we knew it, a pattern had developed. She would misbehave, we would ground her and restrict her from taking part in after-school activities for a short time, and then the pattern would repeat itself. The discipline measures we took didn't seem to faze her. And what's interesting is we thought her problems paled in comparison to other teenage adolescents.

One of the last images I have of our time in Laurel Hollow comes from the time that Mike and I took Heather to the city park near our house. We took her somewhere neutral so we could air out our concerns and so she could do the same. We were trying to be as democratic as possible with her while standing our ground.

It was a bright, sunny day. Even though we needed sunglasses to protect our eyes from the glare of the sun, it was unseasonably cold. Mike and I sat on an empty bleacher seat, and Heather sat between us. I felt like a moderator. I sat back and listened as Mike did most of the talking. It made sense because Heather listened to him more than me. We talked to her about her behavior and our concern that she was putting herself in harm's way. We talked about boys, sex, appropriate behavior for a girl her age and the importance of making good decisions. There we were, the three of us, working through the challenges that accompany early teenage life.

It wouldn't be long after that talk in the park that our time living in Laurel Hollow would come to a close. And as it did, little did we know that one of the neighborhood boys, who was there the night Heather and her girlfriends got caught teasing the young men from Heather's bedroom window, would re-enter our lives a few years down the road in a very destructive way—so destructive, it's beyond our comprehension.

With the challenges that occurred in Laurel Hollow behind us, so we thought, we moved to Kensington. Also, Mike and I decided I'd take time off from work because, for me, even though I had only worked on the musical for a year, it had become all-consuming. Our thought was that taking a break from the development of the musical would allow me the opportunity to be more available to Heather, and I'd be more able to help the kids with their studies and extracurricular activities.

I remember the moment I told Roland I was stepping back because it emotionally stung. I didn't want to take a break. But I had a gut feeling I needed to.

When I spoke to Roland, it was the day before Mike and I moved into the new house. I called him and said, "Roland, I'm so sorry, but I think I'm going to have to step back. Mike and I bought a house in Kensington…and for now—"

"Oh! Heavens no! What?! Jen! This doesn't make sense! What about—"

"Roland! Stop! Just listen to me for a minute. Mike and I are very worried about Heather. We're putting our family first, Roland. This is only temporary! Just give me some time. I'll keep in touch and try to limit the break."

"Oh! Jen! Please rethink this. What am I going to tell the team? We've come so far! Now that the musical score, script and choreography are complete, we just need to work on costume and set design, and—"

"Just tell them I'll be back. It's temporary! Until then, move forward. And maybe slow down a bit..."

"But—"

"No buts, Roland. I have to do this for Heather. I'll be in touch. I promise."

The following day, we moved into our current house. We also transferred the kids from the Laurel Hollow school system to the Kensington school system. And we experienced a reprieve for a few years regarding Heather's rebellious behavior.

Mike and I both agreed that having me home full-time once again seemed to help, and as a result, I ended up tabling the musical for four years. During the four-year break, everyone went on to other projects. And even though I distanced myself from the project, I stayed in close contact with Roland, but I focused my time and energy on my family.

During my hiatus, the kids flourished, and I was more involved with their schooling than ever before. Like years past, I helped them get to school, and I helped them with their studies. And in addition, I attended all of their after-school functions.

Regarding after-school functions, Jerry found a good part-time job he focused on while the girls got involved in extracurricular activities. And since it's been several years since the kids were in school, the memories of the girl's after-school activities come back like rapid firing paparazzi camera flash lights. *Click...click...click...click...*I see Sam. She's playing a clarinet solo at a school concert. *Click...*She's singing at a school concert. *Click...*She's singing *Bring on the Rain* by Jo Dee Messina at a junior high talent show, and we're laughing along with her as the DJ accidentally plays the real Jo Dee Messina version instead of the backing track while Sam stands there holding the mic singing the song. The crowd erupts in applause thinking the voice they hear is Sam until the DJ figures out his mistake and turns off the music. There she is, my beautiful Samantha, cringing yet smiling and making a cute, silly face at the crowd as if she's saying, "Yeah! That's me singing! Not!" The DJ fixes his mistake, starts the backing track, and Sam sings. We get to hear her beautiful voice, and when she's done singing, the crowd erupts in applause again because she sang so well! There we are…Jerry, Heather and me grinning ear to ear and proudly clapping along with the crowd. *Click*…I see Sam playing volleyball at a tournament. *Click*…I see her playing softball at a softball game. *Click*…I see Heather singing…I can't see any other memories at the moment of Heather. I just can't. Wait…I can see her and Sam jumping rope at a jump rope tournament. Oh my God! They're doing the *tornado* jump rope move in unison! Yes! Look at them go! This is *so* cool! Those are *my* girls! They're amazing! Wow…so many beautiful moments. *POOF!* The multiple camera flash lights stop.

It wasn't until Heather started her junior year of high school that the problems started once again. By then, Jerry had graduated from high school, and Sam was a sophomore. And I had resumed development of *Laced*.

Heather became increasingly moody and easily agitated. Her moods were so extreme she even joked with her best friend Lexi that she and Lexi had a *bipolar* friendship. And even though she laughed and joked with Lexi about their *rollercoaster* friendship, she found no humor in her relationship with Mike and me. And instead, she would talk back to us unabashedly. As her junior year of high school went on, she became more confrontational about anything and everything.

Since Mike and I didn't understand that she had a mood disorder, we were just as confrontational back. For instance, one evening, when I told her she couldn't go out with her girlfriend's, she yelled, "What the hell! Get out of my face! Go work on your fucking perfect musical, Mom!"

I slapped her face and yelled back, "Heather Renee! Don't you *ever* say that again!" I still can't believe I struck her. It pains me when I think about how I reacted. I have a lot of guilt about my behavior. Knowing what I do now, I'm ashamed of myself for not catching on sooner. Regardless, Mike and I couldn't put our finger on it. All we knew was that we had an out-of-control teenager. Simple.

Sam also noticed that Heather was becoming more agitated as time went on. She told me she saw Heather and her high school sweetheart yelling at one another in the school hallway. She said, "Mom! Heather screams at Joel while standing at his locker. It's so embarrassing! It's like she wants everyone to know they have problems or something! What's wrong with her?!" I didn't have an answer.

Around that same time, while trying to get Heather awake and out of bed, I discovered that she was cutting herself. With Heather, it was different. Usually, cutters hide their self-inflicted wounds, not Heather. She cut herself on the outside of her wrist—in plain sight for everyone to see. The cut marks couldn't be hidden with the short sleeve t-shirts she so often wore.

For certain, Mike and I were clueless. We didn't understand what she was going through. The only thing that made sense to us as parents is that we knew something was wrong. How could she cut into her beautiful, delicate skin and make herself bleed? I sat on her bedside and looked at her arms in disbelief. There was my daughter, deathly afraid of needles growing up, with cut marks on top of both of her wrists. The cut marks were horizontal and about two-inches long. And she spaced them apart as if she was decorating her wrists with bangled bracelets. When I asked her about the marks, she clammed up. At that point, we sought counseling. Sadly, it took visible wounds for us to act.

The first counseling session didn't go well. Afterwards, Heather told me she didn't think the counselor listened to her, so she stopped going. I then set her up with another counselor. And again, the counselor didn't seem to be of much help. I even went, at Heather's request, to a few of the sessions.

At one appointment I attended, she told the counselor she was feeling a lot of anxiety. She also said she was having panic attacks. Regardless, she ended up leaving the appointment empty handed. She didn't get what she needed. But I left with a thought I didn't want, the thought that maybe Heather wanted prescription medication. And again, like clockwork, she stopped going to her appointments with the second counselor.

Around this time, she started to lie about her plans for the weekend. On Friday nights, she'd ask me if she could stay the night with her friend Tina. And usually I had no problem with it. Mike and I encouraged the kids to get out, make new friends and have fun.

Well, on one of those occasions, I had a feeling that Heather was up to something so the next day, around noon, I called her. And when I did, she didn't pick up. So I drove over to Tina's house to see what was up. As I drove down the street to Tina's house, what did I see? I saw Heather's vehicle, our old, dark green Jeep Grand Cherokee we'd given her, parked in front of someone else's house, not Tina's. There her Jeep sat— vacant. So I went back home and waited for her to return.

When she eventually returned home, I confronted her about her whereabouts the night before. She didn't argue with me, like I expected. She said instead of going to Tina's house, as promised, she'd parked her Jeep near Tina's house and then walked to Joel's house and spent the night with him. Even though her secret was out, it didn't seem to matter to her.

Unfortunately, her misbehavior continued, and more often than not, Jerry and Sam would get pulled into it. One day, while Jerry was on his way to work, he noticed the Grand

Cherokee sitting vacant in a nearby neighborhood. He called Mike to let him know something was up with Heather. He told Mike that she had abandoned the Jeep, and it was unlocked. And what was scary was that her purse was sitting on the passenger seat—and her keys were in the ignition switch.

Without hesitation, Mike went to look for her. On his way, he called me and said, "Honey, the Jeep's parked in the neighborhood across from us. I don't know where to look, but I'll start somewhere and will call you back." I was beyond frightened. I didn't know if I should call the police or what. I trusted Mike's instincts and waited to hear from him. About ten minutes later, he called me and said, "I found her. I'll tell you what happened when I get home."

I yelled nervously back into the phone, "Oh my God! What the hell's wrong with her? You told her *explicitly* not to stay out long because you two have a flight to catch to Miami in the morning for her *North American Stars* audition!"

Mike replied, "I'll be right there, Jen." And then all I heard was…*click.*

The pattern of Heather marching to the beat of a different drummer continued, and Mike and I grew more and more frustrated. Besides marching to her own beat, she became more distant and more tired as time went on. Her room became a cluttered pile of clothes, shoes, school work, crocheted remnants and new and partially used skeins of yarn and crochet hooks. In addition, there were usually scissors lying on the floor near her bedside—evidence she was still cutting. Sadly, the *unraveling* continued, and we still couldn't put a finger on it. And we couldn't stop it…

GLOOM

The title to Chris Daughtry's 2007 hit song *It's Not Over* eerily nails Heather's senior year of high school. It reminds me, every time I hear it, of the frustrations and challenges Heather faced, and her loved ones, regarding her ever-changing moods and behaviors as she worked her way toward the twelfth grade finish line. The storm that had been brewing for years was picking up speed. And the challenges we faced her junior year were nothing like what was to come.

Her senior year proved to be the most difficult year out of all twelve years of her schooling. In fact, it was so rough, we were afraid she wouldn't graduate. Instead of flourishing, as her siblings and friends did, she isolated herself from anyone and everyone she knew and retreated to her bed. If she wasn't at school, she was in bed. If she wasn't at work, she was in bed. And her sleep schedule was the polar opposite of our sleep schedule. During the day, she slept, and during the night, she stayed up and texted back and forth with Joel—all night long. And she stopped showering regularly. It was painful to see because she'd been so active up to that point. And any counseling she'd received prior didn't seem to help.

I was ignorant to what was happening. I didn't see that depression had glommed onto her like an uninvited invisible dance partner. But it did. And the mood altering monstrosity intermingled with her day in and day out as if she were its victimized partner forced to dance a never-ending gloomy waltz she didn't want to dance.

The image of her dancing the gloomy waltz reminds me that although depression had a hold of her, she attended both her senior homecoming dance and prom. And on both occasions, she looked like a princess. For homecoming, she wore one of Sam's glamourous pageant gowns, an aqua floor length ball gown with a flowy silk chiffon skirt and crystal V-neck bustier. And for prom, she wore a gown she handpicked herself at a nearby bridal boutique. It was an elegant strapless floor length white satin sheath wedding gown with a sweep and a sparkling Swarovski crystal embellished belt. I admit, I thought it was odd she wore a wedding gown to prom, but that was the least of my worries.

She was a senior princess at both high school dances tainted with markings of depression. There they were—the dark markings—evidence of depression's existence, an existence I couldn't see. There it was screaming in my unenlightened face, a face that couldn't see the clues she was dropping, and had been dropping since her junior year, like bread crumbs on an untraveled path—a dying smile, loss of interest in daily activities, irritability, self-harm and the list goes on—and I failed at recognizing the symptoms.

Even though depression had taken hold, we had mother-daughter moments that further clouded my already skewed judgment like the moment she told me how prom night went. It was as if a baseball umpire within my unconscious mind was yelling at me, "Safe!"

There we were—the two of us. She said, "Mom! Joel told me he wants to marry me, and he's going to propose on top of the Empire State Building!" And it was what it was—a mom and a daughter talking about high school romance.

She escaped the binds of depression long enough to get lost in the romantic thought of a wedding proposal. And I relished in it. I saw it as a glimmer of hope. Maybe happiness was just around the corner. Maybe she had been feeling *down* for a while and everything would be okay.

Further clouding my mind was her ability to work. She worked part-time at an ice-cream shop, and the first few weeks on the job, she could handle the demands of both school and work. And she seemed to enjoy the camaraderie of the people she worked with. But about a month in, the pace of the job, and the demands of the customers, stressed her out. And she struggled with getting to work on time. By the time prom came around, her enthusiasm waned to the point she didn't bother to show up at work. So they let her go.

What a year her senior year was. And it stands out in stark contrast to the year before. During her junior year, despite that she was battling a mood altering monstrosity I couldn't see: she was an active member in Show Choir, Chamber Choir, Encore, Madrigals and February Frolics. And she played a part in the school musical *Beauty and the Beast*. And she wrote music and poetry and sang with her friends and family, and she tried out for the *North American Stars Competition* show in four different states. She also entered a televised singing contest and auditioned on air with a local television network in the New York area.

Also, during her junior year, it wasn't uncommon for friends and family to find the girls and me singing and dancing around in our living room on random occasions. We loved to sing and dance while listening to our favorite songs by bands like Heart and Journey. And during those special moments, we'd laugh out loud at how silly we must have looked as we moved around the room and belted out song after song while listening to songs like "Dreamboat Annie," "Crazy on You," and "Wheel in the Sky." And we'd laugh even harder when Clinker got in on the action and crooned along as she watched Sam and I twirl about while Heather sang into a hairbrush as if it were a microphone.

I think about those moments, and I smile. Oddly enough, as Heather's zest for life was fading her junior year, it was a time when she was full of energy, passion and humor. Even though she was mentally spiraling downward, there were moments when she laughed and made jokes. And even though she could become irritable at a moment's notice, once over whatever obstacle it was, she appeared satisfied. At least—that's what this unlearned face saw.

And then came her senior year. When I think back to that year, I see a twelve-month one page academic calendar with nothing but huge red X's splattered everywhere because she missed so many days of school. The staggering number of absences she'd accrued put her at risk of losing credit and not graduating. And it caught up to her. Because of her absences, she had to attend a study hour class on Saturday's. There she was, at the end of the compulsory education ride, and she was shutting down.

I felt like I had to prod her to get to the senior finish line. There I was most mornings before school hastily saying, "Heather...get up! You're going to be late for school, again! Heather...Heather...Heather...pleeeease get up. Sam's already at school!"

At one point, I showed her the student handbook and discussed with her the seriousness of her absences and tardiness. But it didn't matter. It didn't seem to faze her. Instead, she figured out exactly how many days she could miss and how many tardies she could get before there would be any repercussions—my plan backfired.

I remember one morning in particular when Heather was late yet again. I somehow drug myself out of bed, despite that I was home with a cold. I was half asleep and dreary and blurry eyed from the red, thick and syrupy medicine I had taken earlier in the morning. I usually changed clothes before heading out the door, but I didn't feel well and was beyond tired at that point from the effects of the cold medicine. I threw a jacket on over my nightgown, put slippers on my feet, grabbed the box of tissue sitting on my nightstand and stumbled downstairs. I figured that as long as I didn't get pulled over, I'd be okay. If not, I'd have to explain the disheveled look. I opened Heather's door, peeked my head inside her room and said, "Heather. It's time to get up. I'm leaving. If you don't get up, you'll have to deal with it."

I then left her room, turned off the home security system and then sleepily headed to the Jeep. By the time I opened the door to the Jeep, sat down, put the keys in the ignition switch and turned the engine on, Heather walked out and jumped in. And I said nothing. Instead, I opened the garage door. And without paying attention, I backed the Jeep out of the garage. As I did, I heard a loud *CRUNCH!* Heather said, "What was that?"

I looked in the rearview mirror and yelled, "Damn it! I hit one of the garbage cans we put out last night! I have to—"

"You don't have time, Mom. We have to go! I'm going to be late!"

I didn't reply. Instead, with a waste container on its side, garbage strewn about and a Jeep with a smashed in rear light cover, I backed out of the driveway and focused on the road in front of me. And I whisked her off to school hoping I'd get her there in time so she'd at least get credit for showing up.

While she was losing her academic footing at school, she was writing *increasingly* dark lyrics, and she worked on her fashion sketching skills. She also crocheted, just like when she was a little girl. And instead of school books and school supplies lying around her room, crocheted hats, she called beanies, and crocheted hemp necklaces appeared as she made them. Also, during this time, she cried easily and talked about having feelings of guilt. And she would apologize for not being better behaved—and I'd hug her and tell her how much I loved her.

I remember times when I'd lay on her bed next to her comforting her and wondering what to do next. There we lay—

me and my beautiful daughter who was spiraling further into the depressed state she was in—and I couldn't save her. I was naïve. Depression, the mood altering monstrosity that glommed onto my girl, was right there staring at me, taunting me and *soon* it would haunt me.

But before it would haunt me, she dropped out of all extracurricular activities the first semester of her senior year so she could focus on the classes required to meet graduation requirements. And Mike and I supported her decision because she told us her classes and activities were too much and were hurting her more than helping her. We were on board. We knew she was struggling, and we saw how brutal her peers were with her, and we didn't want her subjected to it anymore.

In her junior and senior music classes, she was literally on the sidelines during performances. Even though she'd make it through auditions, and was a member of several elite music groups, she was never out front on show nights. I remember one Show Choir performance in particular when Mike, Sam and I sat up as tall as we could to see over the heads of the people in front of us. When the show started, we leaned forward and intently and anxiously looked for her, especially since she told us her music teacher had given her a major part to sing. When we finally spotted her, we saw that someone had placed her in the back and to the right side of the group. And we could barely see her. It was like she blended into the stage curtains. And in that moment, as in all the other moments, we could see her self-esteem crumbling. And we couldn't fix what had happened.

Yet another incident that happened occurred when she auditioned at a nearby mall. Even though it didn't have to do with school, it was yet another devastating blow at a time when Heather was emotionally fragile and experiencing being shut out by her peers at school. It had worked out that Mike and I sat directly behind the judges at the audition. Act after act performed and then Heather's time to sing came. There she was singing "Complicated" by Avril Lavigne. As she sang, Mike turned to me and whispered, "I can see the scores! The judges gave her all tens!"

I grinned at him and whispered back, "Yes!"

We were ecstatic. She finally had some recognition. Then—sadly—the judges announced that another singer won. It was gut-wrenching to see happen. It seemed Heather couldn't catch a break.

Through it all, we continued to lift her up. It was strange though because she was very gifted as a singer and others continually praised and recognized her for her gift yet it seemed as if a force of some sort held her back. Even in Texas, when she tried out for the *North American Stars Competition* show, my brother said, "No worries. She'll advance to the next round. You'll see!"

Instead, the judge ridiculed her. So when she said she that she was dropping out of her elective classes and extracurricular activities, we supported her decision. It seemed like the right thing to do. We wanted to support her as she expressed her independence. But we were very sad to see her stop singing in school.

And to add insult to injury, her name is missing in the back of her senior yearbook. When she saw that, it hurt her deeply, and it hurt me too. It was like she didn't exist. With her self-esteem hanging by a thread, she hung out with new friends and drank.

One Saturday morning, while we were still in bed, Mike got an early morning call from the dad of one of her friends. I couldn't make out what her friend's dad was saying, but I heard Mike say, "Yes, this is Mike. All right...I'll be right there."

I asked Mike, as he jumped up out of bed, "Who was that?"

As he pulled up his jeans, he said, in a disappointed voice, "It was Dawn's dad. The girls got drunk last night. I guess they were drinking vodka. Anyway, Heather's been vomiting all morning and dropped her phone in the toilet. That's why her dad called. Dawn helped fish her phone out of the toilet and it's drying out. I have to go get her. You going with me?"

"Yeah," I said, in a depleted tone.

I too got out of bed, and I found clothes to wear and got in the Jeep with Mike. On the way to her friend's house, I said, "Mike, I'm worried. What are we going to do?"

He shrugged his shoulders in disappointment and said, "I don't know, Jen. Doesn't she have to work this morning?"

"Yep."

"Okay. Well, since she didn't call in, she has to go."

I didn't respond. Instead, I remained quiet. I was too deep in thought at that point wondering what to do with her. After we picked her up, Mike told her on the drive home, "You have a responsibility, Heather. You're going to work!" She was too sick to say a word, so when we got home, she cleaned up and headed out the door. We heard years later that she called her boyfriend, and he picked her up and they went to his house for the day.

Eventually, she graduated from high school spring of 2008. What a relief. Any grief we went through trying to get her to school didn't matter at that point. She'd earned her diploma. And we were overjoyed.

With her first twelve years of school behind her, she went on a road-trip to California with Sam, her aunt, uncle and cousins. She didn't want to, but Mike and I persuaded to go. Reluctantly, she went. To get to California, the girls first had to fly from New York to Dallas, Texas where my brother lives. Once there, the girls loaded up in my brother's car along with him and the rest of his family and headed out for the long trek west.

According to accounts from family, Heather was on her phone incessantly chatting with her boyfriend. Her relationship with Joel had consumed her, and a trip west wasn't about to stop it. She called me frequently to tell me she wanted to come home. She said she was miserable, but Mike and I encouraged her to go easy on herself, relax a little and enjoy her time with her extended family.

While the girls were out of town, I called an old producer friend of mine who lives in California. She's a producer for a popular TV show that's filmed in Hollywood. I thought maybe she'd want to interview Heather for an intern position I heard she had open, especially since Heather was going to be in her neck of the woods. It seemed like the perfect fit for Heather. She could work during the day where the show is filmed and then pursue her singing career after hours. My friend was extremely kind. But she said it would be in Heather's best interest to get a college degree, first. Admittedly, Mike and I were disappointed to hear her answer. But in time, we discovered what a blessing it was.

After the girl's two-week adventure on the road, they returned to New York. And Heather picked up where she left off with Joel. And the two of them fought more than they ever had before. Her relationship with him was derailing in front of everyone. One moment, he'd pick her up to go see a movie, and the next, she'd be sitting at home telling me and Sam how he'd upset her. By the end of summer, he headed off to Yale. And Heather retreated to her bed.

Her spiral downward happened right when Roland and the team and I had finished costume and stage prop designs and had interviewed and hired the actors and band members for the musical. We were right at the workshop stage and had rented studio space in Upper Manhattan.

Heather wasn't sure if she wanted to go to college, so I encouraged her to take a morning class at Columbia University which was near the studio. She liked my idea and took a photography class. And she seemed to enjoy it. One day, she said, "Mom, I have to take black-and-white pictures, and I don't know what to take pictures of!"

I said, "Honey, stop by the studio! You can meet the cast members and take pictures there! I know Roland and everyone else would love to see you!" She liked my idea and took me up on it.

I remember the first time she came to the studio. I was extremely proud of her, and I wanted to show her off. She knew who Roland was, but she hadn't met the cast, the crew or the band. So when she stopped in, I proudly introduced her to everyone. I know that my face must have lit up as I grinned from ear to ear and said, "Everyone! I have an announcement to make! This is Heather, my daughter! She needs to take pictures for her photography class so if you have any ideas, please let her know. She'll be hanging out with us for a while to get this done!" Heather smiled at me nervously and then mingled with everyone. They were so welcoming. They cheered her on as she walked around and snapped picture after picture of things like the keys on the piano, a random bar stool, the bouquet of Oriental poppies, and the cast in action.

After she met the team, and snapped the pictures she wanted, I took her to a nearby coffee shop. Then, afterwards, she and I temporarily parted ways for a few hours, and I returned to the studio. Upon my return, I relished in the conversations that took place regarding Heather. It was my opportunity to brag. And as I did, several of the team members told me how beautiful she was, and I couldn't agree more! I was so proud of her. She finally seemed to be on her way. She was no longer a fledgling hanging off the nest. Instead, she seemed to have found her wings and was flying.

Then, on a warm fall day, Heather called me while I was at the studio. She asked me if she could come by. After a brief conversation, we decided that we'd meet outside near the automatic doors by the front entrance to the building since she'd taken up smoking. I hated that she smoked, but I wanted to see her, so I agreed.

Without hesitation, I took the elevator down to the first floor. As soon as I got there, I walked down the hallway toward the exit doors. When I got close to the doors, they automatically opened, and I stepped inside a vestibule. There I was, alone, in a small holding area—sandwiched between clear glass doors behind me and clear glass doors in front of me—waiting to see my girl. While I waited for the doors in front of me to open, I could see her. She was sitting on a bench with a stocky young man with black hair sitting next to her, and I noticed that they were both smoking. Before I could think another thought, the doors opened. I hesitantly walked towards Heather before they closed again. And as I walked up to her, I recognized the young man. His name is Matt, and he's one of the neighborhood boy's from Laurel Hollow who showed up at our house the night Heather got into trouble. And I was witnessing the beginning of a torrid love story that would end with disastrous consequences.

LIT

After reconnecting with her childhood friend, Matt, Heather's life turned totally upside down. To begin with, she stopped attending photography class. And the illness that was slowly *corroding* her brain, and that I didn't see, weakened her ability to control herself—and she became reckless.

Her life became a helter-skelter mess and took one unbelievable turn after another. And as she tried to keep up with herself, she somehow pulled me along with her. I remember one day in particular during this time. It was a day when Heather had missed class and randomly showed up at the studio. I was in the middle of a heated argument with Cade, the show's musical director, and Roland when my phone vibrated in my pocket. Her timing couldn't have been better. Roland and Cade were arguing about who was actually the director of the show. I didn't like that there was any confrontation at all, so when my phone rang I immediately picked it up. To my surprise, it was Heather. She said, "Hey, Mom…I'm in the lobby!"

Thankful she saved me from an uncomfortable situation, I said, "I'll be right there!" and then headed her way and left the guys to fight it out. I was glad I had an excuse for escaping their ridiculous argument. And I was excited to see her.

My eagerness to see her came to an abrupt halt the moment I laid eyes on her. I'm ashamed to admit it, but when I saw her, I felt embarrassed and hoped that passerby's wouldn't see her. And—my heart broke.

STACY A. KING

There she was standing alone in the lobby, my beautiful girl, standing there with dirty nails and unkempt hair and clothes that looked they came from her dirty clothes hamper. It was painful to witness. While I looked at her in shock and disbelief, my girl smiled back at me and talked about accidentally sleeping in. Before anyone noticed her, I urged her to go outside with me by pointing to the exit doors and walking away from her, knowing she'd follow me.

Once seated outside, she talked excitedly about her reconnection with Matt. She said, "Mom...he's my true soulmate!"

In response, unable to understand how she *knew* Matt was her soulmate when Joel was her soulmate a few months back, I nodded my head and said, "Uh-huh."

She didn't seem to notice my puzzled look. Instead, she said, "He's gotten into trouble for drunk driving and had other run-ins with the law...and he sold drugs for a while...but he's changed now, Mom! He doesn't do those things anymore!" Despite that he was a good boy now, according to Heather, his old bad boy behavior seemed to attract her.

As she gushed about her renegade sweetheart, I felt myself wither physically. Our eye to eye contact changed as I turned my focus toward the ground beneath my feet. My shoulders and head collapsed under the weight of her revelation. And my mind filled with questions. *What is going on with my girl? When will she wake up? When will she see that this guy is trouble?*

Even though it felt like time stopped, the day Heather told me she was dating Matt, time flew by. And before we knew it, it was December, and she dropped her photography class to avoid a failing grade. With that, she told me she wanted to enroll in beauty school in the spring, even though she didn't have the money to do so. I was glad to hear she had a Plan B. Besides singing, she always wanted to go to beauty school. She loved doing hair and makeup so it made sense. Her dad didn't share in my enthusiasm. Regardless, I talked him into funding her new endeavor. And without realizing it, I had opened Pandora's box.

Not only did I expose her to the world of beauty school, but I exposed her to new evils of the world. And as a result, she gained more than her beauty school education. She also gained a friend who was a stripper and a heroin addict, and Heather herself gained an audience as she too stripped at a local gentlemen's club. While she played with fire, her dream of becoming a *North American Stars Competition* winner shattered, and she grew worse. We also learned that besides drinking and stripping, she tried a variety of street drugs—cocaine, heroin and LSD—and she became a regular pot smoker.

The words: addict, stripping, street drugs, cocaine, heroin and LSD bounce around in my brain still to this day. Not one of the hundred billion nerves that make up the central organ of my nervous system has accepted that Heather was a drug user, or a stripper. Seeing the words on my computer screen come alive, even with emphasis—**addict, stripper, street drugs, cocaine, heroin and LSD**—doesn't work. Caught somewhere inside my skull, they ricochet from lobe to lobe until my brain refocuses elsewhere.

Denial, in all its powerful glory, magically transports my thoughts to a bizarre moment that occurred during Heather's spring semester of beauty school. She went with Matt to see our family doctor regarding the anxiety she said she was experiencing, and then she showed up at the studio with Matt in the shadows. I recall that it was Janelle, our choreographer, who brought them to the practice area. Once she located me, she said, "Look who I found in the lobby, Jen!" As I turned my attention away from the practice stage and toward the sound of Janelle's voice, I saw Heather and Matt standing next to Janelle. Janelle said, "It was nice meeting you, Matt! And Miss Heather...How wonderful to see you again! Stop by more often!" She winked at Heather and then walked away.

I was thrilled that Heather had stopped by yet again but very unhappy to see Matt. Regardless, I had to deal with him. So rather than stay and talk in the practice area, I motioned for Heather and Matt to follow me to the break room. Once in the break room, Heather lost her composure. She complained that the doctor had refused to prescribe her medication. Shaking in frustration, she yelled at me under her breath, "Mom! Dr. Roberts doesn't understand what I'm going through! I neeeed something to calm me down! I don't like him! He didn't listen to me! What am I supposed to do?!"

Caught off guard, and once again hoping that no one would see us, I shrugged my shoulders and said, "I don't know. I'm so sorry." Matt didn't say a word. He remained quiet the entire time which bothered me because I knew he was up to no good and most likely asked her to get some benzos. It didn't work though. And in response to my empty comment, she sat down on the one and only couch that existed in the break room—a black leather studio couch for two—crossed her legs and bounced her right foot up and down nervously for a few minutes and then got up and left the studio with Matt in tow. Rather than cause any upset, I didn't say a word and went back to work.

Honestly, I was glad that Dr. Roberts didn't give her a prescription because once again we were not sure if she was telling the truth. I'm confident the doctor knew Matt and Heather were abusing benzo's or selling it. Sadly, maybe Heather needed something to help calm her nerves, but it was difficult to understand what she did and didn't need. What skewed things even more was that Heather seemed knowledge-able about the sedative when in fact she hadn't taken it before—at least not legally.

Another odd moment that happened that spring—a moment tainted by drugs—occurred late one evening when Heather brought her heroin addicted friend Amber over to our house to get ready to go out on the town. When Heather introduced her, I noticed how frail the young woman was. Not only was she thin from drug abuse, but she talked hurriedly, had bloodshot eyes, tiny pupils and a runny nose. I also noticed how unkempt she was. Her long, straight brown hair was greasy looking, and the clothes she wore—a tight fitting, dingy white tank top, baggy dark blue sweatpants and white flip-flops—looked filthy dirty. Even her hands and feet looked grimy. It was obvious she hadn't showered in days. I felt sorry for her, and concerned.

After Heather introduced her to us, she followed Heather to her room, and eventually, the girls made their way from Heather's room to the full-length mirror in our hallway. They busily talked, and applied makeup, while looking at themselves in the mirror. After they applied their makeup, they went back to Heather's room, changed into skimpy dresses, and then left.

While the girls got ready for the evening, Mike watched TV, and I meandered from room to room full of nervous energy. I was very concerned about what was to come. I even tried to talk to Heather about her plans for the night, but she didn't want to talk. She threw up her hands and said, "Stop! I don't want to hear it, Mom!"

As always, she kept marching to a different drummer doing her own thing how she wanted to do it. She was becoming a danger to herself. And I couldn't protect her from herself. Since Mike and I had no control at that point, we were going to tell her to move out of the house. But before we had the chance to meet with her about it, she moved in with Matt and his family.

While living with Matt and his family, Heather continued her studies at the beauty school. I remember many a day when she'd call me from the school. Each time she called, she'd be in full-blown panic mode. And every time this happened, I'd play off that something was wrong when I picked up my phone. And I'd excuse myself from show practice while on the other end of the phone was Heather saying she was in a bathroom stall at school. She sounded like a caged animal. It was awful being on the other end of the phone while she sobbed and said, "I have to whisper…I'm not supposed to be in here. I don't think I can do this, Mom! I hate it here! And I think the other girls are out to get me…help!" In response, I'd talk her through the panic attack. Once over her fears, she'd stay at school and finish her hours for the day. Then she'd stop by the studio, before heading over to Matt's house, and tell me she wanted to finish beauty school.

I have to admit that it was hard taking her serious during times like these since she had fooled us when she was in grade school. It was hard to deny the panic attacks though, especially since she experienced them elsewhere, like the day I talked her into going with me to the mall. There we were on an escalator gliding downward toward the first floor of the mall when she said, "Mom…I'm not feeling right…Everyone's staring at me. I have to get out of here!" I felt so bad for her. I gently put my hand on her shoulder and told her, "I'm here. It's okay. Let's go." And I helped her exit the mall.

Around the time the panic attacks began, she started tanning every day. Mike and I talked to her about the dangers of tanning, but she refused to listen. Each time I saw her, her skin was darker than the time before. She tanned so much that her skin looked bruised. And any money she made, she spent right away on tanning. It didn't matter to her how bad it was for her health. She did her own thing no matter how harmful it was to her body.

Then there were the times when she'd stop by the studio for a moment only to leave again and go on what she called "a drive." We later learned that when she went on "a drive," she smoked pot while driving on the back roads. That explained why the interior of the old Grand Cherokee started to smell like a skunk sprayed it.

Not only did the Grand Cherokee take on a foul smell, but a smattering of small black holes, created from hot burning ashes, showed up as well on the driver's side seat, and trash filled the vehicle. And food stains and drink spills appeared on the seats and carpet. The deteriorating state of the Grand Cherokee represented her mental scatterings and how out of control she had become.

She had gotten so out of control and reckless that one afternoon, while sitting on the break room sofa at the studio, she stretched the earring hole in each one of her earlobes. When I asked her, "What are you doing?"

She replied, "I'm gauging my earlobes...I'm going up a few sizes."

All I could eek out was, "Heather!" as I sat and watched in horror as she tore, stretched and pulled at the skin of one her earring holes while pushing a plug into it. When she tore at the second earring hole in her other earlobe, I couldn't contain myself, and I yelled, "Heather Renee! Stop that!" But she ignored me. In retrospect, I think she was high. I had to leave the room to keep from throwing up and to stop anyone from entering. It was beyond disturbing to watch. I felt fortunate that the break room was empty except for Heather and me and that no one ventured by during this horrific time. Even though we needed help, I wanted to hide, and I did. After Heather left, I returned to the set and acted as if nothing happened.

It was right after the earlobe incident I learned that she had been stripping. I was in bed one evening reading over the Playbill magazine ad that Roland and our advertising executive John had drafted for our upcoming Off Broadway debut; Heather had come by the house and crawled into bed with me. She said, "Mommy...I have to tell you something."

I knew something was up because she hadn't called me *Mommy* for years. While she lay there, with my white down comforter pulled up to her chin and her head on Mike's pillow,

I casually looked over at her and replied, "Okay, what's going on?"

As I laid the Playbill ad down on the bed next to me, she whispered, "Wellll...I've been...I've been doing something bad."

Unprepared for what was to come next, I asked her again, "What's going on, Heather?"

She replied, "You know...Amber?"

"Yes." I replied.

"She's a stripper."

"Oh, Heather..."

"And you know how you work on a stage?"

"Yeah...well...it's just been a faux practice stage until now...but yeah."

"Well, I've been working on a stage too."

"What are you talking about?"

"I've been stripping, Mommy."

Immobilized by her words, as if hit by a stun gun, I couldn't talk. Even though I sat still, dazed by the words she uttered, things around me shifted and moved. My peripheral vision, unaffected, saw the Playbill ad fall off the bed as she sprang up from the bed and sat Indian style facing me. "But it's okay, Mom! I knew it was wrong so I quit!" Shocked at her revelation, I froze. And she waved her hand in front of my face and said, "Mommy...Mom...hello?!"

The worry in her voice snapped me back to reality, and I grabbed hold of her and hugged her. While embracing her, she said, "Matt was the one who wanted me to strip." I pushed her off of me and said, "Heather Renee! What?! Thank God you're okay! Don't ever do that again! Promise me!" She nodded, grabbed hold of me and sobbed.

Rocked with concern and fear by what she'd self-disclosed, I found solace in that moment because I knew she was safe in my arms. But to this day, I still can't believe Matt put her up to that.

What a horrible idea. He didn't love her. He used her and abused her. But it didn't matter. She continued to live with him and his family.

During this unsettling—volatile—time in her life, she got hired on at an area fast-food restaurant. But that too didn't last long. She said she couldn't handle the stress of the work hours and her school responsibilities so she quit. What *really* was going on was a lot of partying, self-medicating and sleeping in wherever the party ended.

And since she couldn't hold down a job, she'd stop by the studio with Matt and ask me for money. I didn't want anyone at the studio to see the state she was in, so I would hand her whatever cash I had each time this happened. I noticed, each time she asked for a handout, that Matt didn't seem bothered by it. Eventually, I stopped giving her money because Mike, Jerry, Sam and I had agreed, during a family meeting, to not give her money anymore. But it wasn't easy.

Heather and Matt were getting by off of the charity of others. And they were in a horrible cycle. He would find work and then not long after get fired and the pattern would repeat. And Heather struggled with herself to make it to school and earn the hours required to graduate from beauty school.

As out of control as Heather's life had become, she'd find time to go on short fishing excursions with Matt. They liked to fish at Crystal Lake, and they also liked to fish at a nearby hidden creek they told me they had discovered. Besides fishing, I learned that they were getting high. On one occasion, after a fishing trip the day before, they stopped by the house to share their experience with me. Matt showed me a picture on his phone, a picture of Heather. He flipped open his phone and said, "Look at this, Mrs. Stein! She scared the shit out of me yesterday!"

When I looked at the photo, I couldn't believe my eyes. It was a photo of Heather sitting on a boulder surrounded by angry whitewater waves that could have knocked her off of the big rock in one swell swoop. I gave Matt back his phone and replied, "I wouldn't have gone out there either! What were you thinking, Heather?"

"It wasn't that scary!" she said laughing. "The hard part was getting out to the boulder!"

"Yeah…whatever, Heather! That was fuckin' crazy!" Matt replied.

Heather gave him the eye as if she was telling him not to cuss around me. I didn't care. I was more worried about her than I was about Matt and his foul language. All I knew was that she had to be very daring to do something like that, or very high.

If Heather and Matt were not fishing, they were partying, and another pattern ensued when it came to their partying. She'd stop by our house to get ready for a party, and Matt would wait in the living room for her. Even though I wasn't comfortable with him, and didn't trust him, I'd try to make small talk. What I was really doing was trying to get details about their plans for the evening just in case Heather needed help later that same night. Once she was ready to go out, they'd head out for the night. I remember lying in bed night after night worrying about where she was. I also wondered whose company she was in and what they were doing. My gut instinct told me she wasn't in good hands.

I know that Matt was verbally abusive. I also know he shoved her. Other than that, Heather said he didn't physically abuse her. I've always had my doubts though, especially based on what I know about how he treated her. For example, while out running errands one day, my phone rang. It was Heather, and she was crying. Through her tears, she asked, "Where are you at?"

I said, "I'm almost to the house. What's going on?"

Still crying, she said, "I need to talk. I'm at the house."

I told her I'd be right there. And we both hung up. A few minutes later, I pulled into the driveway. And there she was with mascara running down her face, sitting on the front step smoking a cigarette. I knew whatever was going on had to do with Matt. Sure enough, it did. When I sat on the step beside her, she told me that Matt had got angry and as he drove Heather from Laurel Hollow to Kensington, he swerved back and forth across the highway as he yelled at her. Still trembling from the incident, she said, "I told him he was scaring me and to stop the car! He wouldn't, Mom! After I kept yelling at him, he finally pulled off the road and parked at the church down the street from our house. And then, he jumped out of the car, pulled me out of my seat, and screamed at me as loud as he could! He clenched his hand into a fist and acted like he was going to hit me…like this!"

She clenched her right hand into a fist and acted like she was going to hit me to show me how he was behaving. Feeling uneasy, I said, "Stop! Heather…I get it." And I pushed her hand away from me.

"It was so embarrassing, Mom! People were leaving the church just then! A guy driving by rolled his window down and asked if everything was okay. Matt quit shaking his fist at me and said, 'Yeah…no problems. Thanks, man!' He then told me to get back in the car!" Still visibly shaking, and with eyes wide open, she continued to talk and said, "Mom! I was so scared! He looked like the Incredible Hulk! He fuckin' scared me! I wasn't gunna get back in the car! I walked home instead! I'm so pissed!"

I didn't know what to say, so I threw my arm around her and said, "I'm so sorry, Heather." Before I could say another word, she looked at her phone, dialed his number and called him. I let go of her in surprise and listened as she told him she forgave him. By the end of the night, she was back with him at his house.

And the cycle would repeat. Not only was I concerned about her boyfriend's behavior, but I was worried about her behavior too. I thought to myself that if she wasn't careful, she could end up in serious trouble, and there was trouble coming…

DERAILED

A s I continue to write, it seems harder to concentrate, especially when I think about what Heather did to herself. I sit. I stare at the computer screen. I get up and get a cup of coffee, and I repeat. My mind hits roadblocks as I journey through the swirling debris of memories, and then I land on an image that my brain can focus on at the moment, the image of me, the lone ballet dancer with tattered and torn ballet slippers gliding across the stage timidly singing in the *Opera Show of Us* while holding up the *stained glass of us*. Damn it! There's a problem though. My ballet slipper, on my right foot, is hung up on something. I try to pull my foot free, but I can't. My slipper has a jagged tear in it. And whatever it's caught on has brought me to an abrupt stop. With my ballet slipper adhered to the floor, I tug and pull at the slipper. And I try to maintain my balance while holding onto the *stained glass of us*. I look down at my foot and frantically move it about. I continue to tug and pull at the slipper hoping it will break loose, but to no avail. I can't seem to get free. I keep tugging…and at last; I feel the slipper give. But instead of breaking loose from the snag on the stage floor, the slipper stays put. As I tug and pull at the slipper, the satin ribbon ties attached to the ballet slipper—that were neatly wrapped around my ankle—loosen, but not enough. And they're keeping my foot *imprisoned* within the slipper. I don't give up. I keep tugging until I feel the ribbons loosen even more. And now, they hang precariously from my foot, and I have a tangled mess! I attempt, one last time, to free myself by pulling the *stained glass of us* in toward my heart with both hands and springing my lower body up into a wicked pirouette, a pirouette that rips my foot loose from the slipper. Finally, I'm free.

As I unravel from my pirouette, free at last from whatever was stopping me from typing the words I type, and with the *stained glass of us* safely in my grip, I'm reminded that Heather's behavior spun out of control on a hot July night in 2009. I remember that Mike was out of town. I had gone to bed and was sleeping lightly, as usual, just in case Heather might need help during the night. And sure enough, my phone rang. I picked it up on the first ring and said, "Heather?"

It wasn't her. It was Matt, and he said, "An ambulance has taken Heather to the hospital. She overdosed."

As I tried to focus and pull myself out of the sleep fog I was in, I slowly replied, "What hospital?" And then…I frantically jumped out of bed and got dressed. I called Jerry and told him that Heather was being taken to the hospital. I then yelled at Samantha, who was asleep in her bed, "Sam! We have to get to the hospital!"

As I ran down the stairs to the garage, she caught up with me. With my attention solely focused on getting to the hospital, I didn't see that she was half dressed until she got into the Jeep. As she bent over to put her tennis shoes on her feet, she said, "What's going on, Mom? Is it Heather?"

I responded, "Yes, sweetie…it is." And I drove to the hospital as fast as I could.

Once there, Sam and I briskly walked through the automatic doors that opened into the emergency room waiting area. And we headed straight for the front desk. When the attendant asked what she could do for us, I said, nervously, "My daughter, Heather Stein, is here."

The attendant looked at her computer. And then she, casually, replied, "Yes, she's in the trauma center. Please have a seat. We'll tell her you're here."

I looked at Sam with a puzzled look and then back at the attendant and said, "My God! Why can't we go back there? I'm her mom! And this is her sister!" And then it hit me. It didn't matter that we were Heather's family. She was over eighteen years of age. She had rights.

As the reality of the situation set in, the attendant said, "Sorry. Please have a seat." I didn't argue with her. Instead, looking wounded—as if we'd lost Heather—Sam and I walked over to a set of chairs and sat down. Jerry, and my *then* daughter-in-law Amber, showed up within minutes, and they had my eleven-month-old granddaughter, Gabby, in tow. Samantha's boyfriend Curt also showed up. There we were, the six of us—sitting, waiting, confused, sad and lost—wondering what Heather had done to herself. I had already called Mike at that point, so he was sitting in Colorado worried and wondering, as we were, about what was next. We all sat with bated breath and cell phones in hand waiting for something… anything…and waiting more…

Time crawled…and I felt sick to my stomach. And I didn't want to, but I saw other people waiting for someone to call their name. There was a young couple with a toddler. I noticed how unkempt the toddler was. She was dirty and didn't have shoes on. Then my mind raced back to why I was there.

After waiting for what seemed like hours, we saw Matt and his buddy walk into the ER. It seemed strange, but he *was* her boyfriend. Regardless, we didn't want to see him, and we didn't want him to see us. Therefore, we didn't move, and we didn't say a word. And it worked. He walked right by us. When he got to the nurses' station, the attendant unlocked the trauma room doors, and both young men walked through the doorway and disappeared. I was mad! I stood up, walked over to the nurses' station and said, "I've been waiting to see Heather Stein! Why did you let them in? I'm her Mother!"

The nurse said, "Heather's been asking for her boyfriend, so I let him in."

I couldn't believe it. I was incredulous. I said, "She's more concerned about seeing her boyfriend?!"

With that, the nurse flipped a switch and unlocked the trauma room doors. She said, "Okay, you can go back now." I didn't mess around. While Sam stayed behind, I faced the doors and then almost ran through them trying to get to Heather.

I don't know where Matt's friend went, but by the time I got to Heather's room, Matt was the only one visiting with her. There was my girl, in a hospital gown, sitting in a reclining position on an emergency room bed with a white sheet covering her from the waist down. And Matt was sitting on her left side. I noticed that Heather didn't seem to know I was there. It was painful. I pulled up a chair and sat on the right side of her bed. There we were.

While looking at her, I asked Matt what happened. He said, "She took a bottle of painkillers."

I didn't respond. I was in shock that Heather seemed to be more concerned about her boyfriend at the moment than herself. Even though she wasn't in a good state of mind, I expected her to be—I was in denial. Then, for whatever reason, he got agitated and said, "Your Mom didn't help you, Heather!" He then looked at me and yelled, "You didn't help her!"

I glared at him in disbelief. And my blood pressure rose like liquid mercury rises in a glass thermometer when dipped in boiling sugar. I was furious he was unleashing his frustrations out on me while my daughter laid there on an emergency room hospital bed.

He then stood up, clenched his fists and leaned in towards me—over Heather's hospital bed. Heather, weak from the pain pills she took, said, "Sit down, Matt. Stop."

As the hair on my neck stood up, I saw someone in the doorway. I looked up long enough to see it was an officer who was observing the situation. But I didn't care. My blood must have been boiling. I was mad that Heather was in this situation and mad that I was being blamed for it. It hurt me at a visceral level. I have a lot of guilt about what I did next, but instead of recoiling, I stood up and yelled, "Go ahead! Hit me!"

Matt hollered, "She's messed up like you!"

I hollered back, "Hit me!"

He then huffed and walked out of Heather's room. I tried to gather myself, and I sat back down. Shortly after, a male orderly walked into the room and told me that Matt was outside yelling obscenities at a police officer and that it looked like he was drunk. He also said Matt wasn't allowed to come back inside. I shook my head in disgust and thanked the orderly for the information. And for a moment, I sat in a hospital emergency room, alone, with my beautiful girl.

Heather's ER nurse, who I hadn't met yet, walked in and sat down next to Heather. What happened next breaks my heart every time I think about it. The nurse asked Heather, "Do you know why you're here?"

Heather said, "Yes."

The nurse said, "Do you want to talk to someone about what happened and why you did what you did?"

Again, Heather said, "Yes."

In response, the nurse handed Heather a clipboard with a document attached to it titled **<u>APPLICATION FOR VOLUNTARY ADMISSION</u>**. The nurse then read, out loud, the verbiage on the application and then squeezed the clip at the top of the board and pulled the document from its grip. She then flipped the document over and read Heather the **<u>RIGHTS</u>**

OF VOLUNTARY ADMISSION verbiage printed on the backside of the document.

When I realized what Heather was doing, I blurted out, "Heather! Do you know what you're signing?"

She didn't look at me. But the nurse did. And I understood the nurse in that moment when she looked me in the eye. She was telling me, telepathically, "Mom, it's her decision."

I felt sick to my stomach. There was nothing I could do. Heather was admitting herself to the psych ward and didn't even know it. It was horrible. I couldn't stop her.

After the nurse read Heather her rights, she asked her to sign the document at the bottom of the page, then flipped the form back over to the front page and re-secured it with the clip. She then filled in the blanks for Heather on the front page and asked for her signature again. Heather did as she asked. As soon as she finished signing her name, the nurse took the clipboard and pen from Heather. And just like that, Heather admitted herself for the first time to a hospital behavioral health unit. And I feared what was to come.

While I internally cringed at what was happening, the nurse left the room with the clipboard and pen in hand. And that was that. Heather wasn't coming home, and I didn't know what to do. I had a son and daughter to inform, who were sitting out in the waiting room, and a husband to call.

While my brain tried to soak in what was happening, I lingered awhile. I couldn't remove myself from her side. And what followed next disturbed me, and the pain was almost too much to bear. She didn't utter a word. Instead, she picked up the corded room phone next to her bedside and pressed the buttons on the telephone keypad. And then, she held the phone up to her right ear. Within seconds, she pulled the phone away from her ear and pressed the buttons again. So I asked her, "Who are you trying to call?"

She didn't respond. Instead, she continued to press the buttons on the keypad. And all I could hear was *click...click...click - click...click...click...click.* After entering whatever phone number she was entering, she lifted the phone up to her ear again and listened. I watched in dismay. And any hope I had that she was okay evaporated in the emergency room air.

I tried again to make contact with her. I said, "Heather, who are you calling, sweetie?"

And again, she didn't respond. All I got was *click...click...click - click...click...click...click.* And again, she held the phone up to her ear.

Devastated by what I was witnessing, I stood up and leaned over her bed. I knew something had gone horribly wrong. I softly kissed her head and said, "Heather...I love you. Mom's leaving now."

She didn't say a word. When I walked out of the room, she was still pressing buttons. And my heart broke unlike it had ever broke before. I gathered my family from the waiting room, and we left the hospital hoping to avoid her irate boyfriend.

READY OR NOT!
HERE I COME!

As I aged, I never really gave much thought to mental illness. It wasn't really talked about at home or in school. I faintly remember, back in the '70s, over-hearing my parents talk about the movie *One Flew Over the Cuckoo's Nest* starring Jack Nicholson. They seemed highly intrigued by it, so I eavesdropped. But when their eyes met mine, and they realized I was listening in, they stopped talking about it. Their guarded behavior taught me, at eight years old, that mental illness was something people didn't talk about.

The only other memory I can recall from my childhood that pertains to mental illness comes from when I was in high school. My mom gave me an old suitcase. She told me it belonged to my grandma who I call *Grandmama*. She said Grandmama was allowed to bring only one piece of luggage with her when she was admitted to a long-term hospital back in the '50s, and this was the piece of luggage she chose. After she died there, a nurse gave it to my mom who then wanted to pass it down to me. When I asked her for more information, she said, "Jen, sometimes people have emotional problems. Someday, we'll talk about it more. For now, just know Grandmama would want you to have it." I didn't pry more. Whatever happened to my Grandmama wasn't talked about. Instead, it was kept hush.

It wasn't until the '90s, when I had a family of my own, that I paid any attention to mental illness. And it took someone famous to catch my attention. I found myself captivated by a national news story on TV. The story was about Margot Kidder, the actress who played the part of Lois Lane in the movie *Superman,* and her battle with bipolar disorder. But when the program was over, I didn't give it another thought. There I was, an adult by then, raising a family of my own, clueless about mental illness.

So the picture in my mind, of mental illness, was blurry, and the topic seemed taboo. Little did I know, while I watched Margot Kidder's challenges with mental illness unfold before the public eye, that years later I'd become intimate myself with the world of mental illness. And the hazy image that existed in my mind—of brain sickness—would become glaringly clear.

Like a game of childhood tag with the echoes of "Ready or not...here I come!" mental illness made its presence known when Heather admitted herself to the psych ward. I could no longer ignore its blatant reality. There it was. There she was. And there I was standing in a hospital dizzy with confusion about what was happening.

The next morning, I called Roland and told him I wouldn't be able to make it to work that day. He was wonderful. He knew we were having problems with Heather, but he didn't pry. Instead, he said, "Jen, hang in there. I'm here for you and Mike. I mean it. If you need anything, just let me know." With that, Sam and I, tired and bleary-eyed, headed back to the hospital to see her. By then, she was a patient on the seventh floor—a floor I didn't know existed.

I recall having bizarre thoughts and feelings. After all, I never thought I'd be going to a psych ward to visit my daughter. And for the first time, questions that revolved around mental illness filled my mind. *What type of treatment is she undergoing? What medications are they giving her? How will she respond to me?*

Regardless, I had a daughter to tend to. But before Sam and I could see her, we had to sign in at the nurses' station. Then we had to wait…and wait…and wait some more.

I noticed that the office procedure on the seventh floor was well organized. In contrast, the seventh floor waiting room lacked attention. There were only three chairs. And there couldn't have been more than an inch of space between each one. Not only was the seating arrangement sparse, but only one chair was vacant. An older man and woman, who looked like they'd seen better days, sat on the other chairs. Sam and I had no place to sit together and no privacy while we waited. We ended up standing the entire time. I was too nervous to sit down anyway.

Besides feeling nervous, I felt so raw and vulnerable as we stood there looking at a security door that had a small window in it. All I wanted was to put my arms around my daughter and tell her how much I loved her. But time seemed to have stopped while Sam and I waited…and waited more.

Finally, I saw my daughter's perfect, beautiful round face in the window. There she was. She looked innocent as she looked at us from behind the window, with her big blue eyes. And there Sam and I were—worn, innocent, scared and clueless—looking at her.

When the automatic door, controlled by a nurse at the nurses' station, unlocked and swung open, I saw a long hallway in front of me with hospital rooms to the left and right. And much to my surprise, about ten feet from the doorway, there was a bold red line on the floor that looked like a finish line. Heather pointed to it and said, "I can't cross it. Patients can't cross the red line." I saw several other patients standing there a few inches from the red line waiting to see their loved ones too.

It all seemed so alien to me. The movie *One Flew Over the Cuckoo's Nest* bolted like a lightning strike through my mind. I felt apprehensive regarding the other patients. Again, questions flooded my mind. *Am I going to see people drugged up and aimlessly wandering the ward? And am I going to see people yelling?* Because that was the only thing I knew. Shame, stigma and fear blurred the image I had of mental illness. I remember, as Sam and I walked towards Heather, I felt like running. I wanted to grab her and take her home. But I couldn't—at least not yet anyway.

THE ETERNAL ESCAPE

Four days after Heather attempted suicide, as the sun climbed the dark sky and spilled its egg yolk colored morning glow over New York, Roland called me and said, "Jen? Are you up?"

Without caffeine coursing through my veins yet, and a phone cradled between my left ear and my shoulder while I scooped coffee grounds out of a jar into a coffee filter with my right hand, I sleepily replied, "Yeah. What's up?"

Unfettered by my lackadaisical reply, Roland said, "Jen! I have fantastic news! *Laced* is going national! It's still not Broadway yet, but that's next, girl!"

Thrilled and fully awake by the news, yet tempered by what was going on with Heather, I replied, "Oh my God! Roland! What? Are you serious? What wonderful news! I don't know what to say!"

"You don't have to say anything, Jen! We still have a lot of work ahead of us, especially now that we'll be touring, but there's no stopping us now! And...I know you have a lot going on with Heather."

"Yeah. We sure do. What am I going to do?"

"What do you mean?"

Before I could stop myself, I spewed my frustrations out on poor Roland. I muttered, "I have to help Heather first! Shit! I can't...I shouldn't talk about this."

"Then don't."

"Roland...Heather's psychiatrist, at the hospital, called us in for a meeting yesterday. Heather was there too. My girl has major depression *and* generalized anxiety disorder. And she's taking meds now...and she's undergoing therapy. The doctor asked me and Mike if Heather can move back in with us."

"Uh-huh..."

"She really never left, so it makes perfect sense. She just sleeps over at Matt's house on and off anyway. I mean...when they're fighting, she stays with us. And you know...if they're getting along, she stays at his parent's house."

"Okay..."

"The doctor also told us that besides medication and talk therapy, she has to stop self-medicating and partying and focus on school. You should have seen her expression, Roland!"

"Really?"

"Oh, my God! She glared at me and Mike like all of this is our fault or something! And she glared at the doctor too. I think she's upset with her. The last thing she wants to do is move back in with us. She doesn't think she has a problem. She wants to go right back into the arms of Matt. But that can't happen right now. The doctor said she won't sign Heather's hospital discharge paperwork until Heather agrees to abide by the rules. So...she's still at the hospital!"

"Wow! I'm so sorry. I don't know what to say. The good news is that you don't have to worry about *Laced*. I've got this! And lean on Mike, I know he's there for you! Things will work out. And I'm here for you too. Jen...Heather will figure this out! She's just a kid."

"I know. You're right. She is. She'll come to her senses here soon, I hope!"

"She will! Well, I'll let you go for now so you can share the news with Mike. I'll be in touch later today with details! Chicago's first! Look out Chicago! And you! Lift your head up, Jen! Your girl's coming home. And you've got a musical that's going places!"

"Yes! Yes! I do! Thank you, Roland! What would I do without you? I love you, my friend. Talk soon…"

And with that, we both hung up. Mike, who was back in town by then, had been standing next to me when Roland called so when I hung up the phone, he asked, "What was that all about?"

Smiling for the first time since Heather admitted herself to the hospital, I said, "Mike! You'll never believe it!"

"Believe what?"

Jumping into his arms, I happily screamed, "*Laced* is going on tour! We're going national!"

"Oh, honey! This is the best news! I'm so proud of you!" he said as he gently grabbed my face with both of his hands and kissed me.

We embraced one another and kissed unlike we'd ever kissed before. There we were. We must have looked like Patrick Swayze and Jennifer Grey in the movie *Dirty Dancing*. At least it felt that way. And then, with lips locked in celebration, the phone rang. Mike pulled away from me while I answered the phone. It was Heather, and she was calling to tell me she was being discharged from the hospital. She must have told the doctor she would abide by the rules. As ecstatic as I felt about Roland's news, I didn't have time to think about *Laced*. Instead, I had a daughter that needed me, and I needed her. With that, Mike and I headed straight to the hospital.

When Mike and I got to the hospital, the parking garage was full so Mike dropped me off at the first entrance he could find. I jumped out of the Jeep as fast as I could and made my way to the elevator doors that were waiting for me. As they opened, I ran to get inside the moving enclosure before the doors closed, and just as I made my way in and turned to face the parking lot, I saw Mike. He was still parked in front of the entrance. A smile let loose across my face as the doors slid shut.

I could barely contain myself during the ride up to the seventh floor. I felt elated. My girl was going home for the first time since being admitted to the behavioral health unit, and I had a show that was making its debut at a professional venue in New York City. When the elevator doors opened, I burst out of the doors. And then reality hit me as the nauseous hospital smell that reeked of sick patients and cleaning fluids hit my nostrils.

I temporarily forgot the awful smell as soon as it hit my senses because I was on a mission, a mission to get my girl. When the elevator reached the seventh floor, and the doors opened, there she was...standing there...free. I should have been ecstatic I was taking her home, but instead, I felt frightened. I also had a feeling of vulnerability and dread wash over me. Heather would no longer be safe in the confines of the hospital. She was free to harm herself once again, and I was *powerless* to stop her. I wanted to scream at the doctors and nurses, "Stop! Don't you understand? She doesn't want to live! Help us! You must keep her and protect her! What are you doing to my girl, and my family? This is a death sentence!"

I remember when she saw me, she briefly hugged me, and asked, "Where's Dad?"

I said, "Oh, honey! He's trying to find a parking spot and then will be right up."

She looked at me with eyes begging me to get her out of the building as fast as I could as if the building was giving way to a massive sinkhole and was crumbling beneath her feet. She said, "Mom! I can't wait that long. Get me out of here!"

Rather than cause any upset, I said, "Okay. Maybe we'll see him on our way out. Let's go!" And just like that, without saying another word, we both got on the seventh floor elevator as soon as the doors opened. I felt relieved when the doors closed because, at least for a moment, she was contained. While we rode down to the first floor, I sent Mike a text and told him we'd had a change of plans and that I'd meet him at the Jeep.

Just as I finished texting Mike, the elevator that Heather and I were in came to a rest on the first floor. As it did, Heather scrambled to get out it before the doors fully opened, and she headed down a random hallway. I yelled at her, "Wait! Heather! That's not the way!" She wouldn't listen to me and instead quickened her pace. I sprinted to catch up to her and to slow her down and get her headed the right direction.

By the time I caught up to her, I was out of breath. Panting, I said, "Heather! You're okay. Slow down! I can't walk as fast as you!"

She didn't speak. But she slowed down enough, we looked somewhat normal. As we walked through the sterile, tunnel like hospital hallways, she said with wild eyes, "I need to get out of here! I hate it here! Get me out of here!" It was like she'd been a caged animal. Our exit from the hospital had become eternal. The hallways became torturous to both of us. The closer we got to the exit door, the sicker to my stomach I felt. I knew I had no control—and I couldn't save her from herself.

As we continued to walk through the maze-like hallways, Heather's pace quickened once again. And I anxiously tried to keep up. She asked repeatedly, "Where's the exit?! Where's the exit, Mom?!" Finally—and against my will—we saw the exit doors. I couldn't believe Heather was being released. And at that moment, everything seemed effortless. There were no people in the hallways to hinder our escape. The automatic doors slid open without hesitation. And just like that, Heather reentered the world.

THE CALLS

D amn it! My thoughts come to a halt. And at a dizzying pace they rewind…and I'm back at the one place I don't want to be. There she is…there's my girl. Wait! I don't want to go there—not yet! I'm not strong enough. My three-pound brain, that absorbed what I saw, remains prisoner to the shock of it all. No one, not even Mike, Jerry, Sam, Roland or my mother can see the damage I incurred the day I found Heather. Instead, all that anyone sees is my physical absence. And while they all focus on my disappearance, I'm fighting within myself to keep the memory of the day I found Heather at bay. And by keeping my distance from those closest, I hope to keep the memory of the *normal* Jen alive for them. I don't want them to see the Jen who has become nothing but a physical shell of herself.

While I try to push the memory from that day back into the confines of the micron-sized brain cells that taunt my psyche, I'm left with little else. My days are filled with the bare minimum, and other days are filled with even less. I shower, shave my legs, get dressed, eat, try to at least smile when I'm around Mike and the kids—and I sleep. But even doing the bare minimum wears me down because the beast that keeps dragging me back to that moment won't relent.

As I wither inside this psychological hell hole, I grab hold of the ballet dancer within, a dancer with one ballet slipper on at this point who lives within a shell-shocked soul. And I hang onto her with all my might. And somehow, despite that she's now damaged goods herself—with raw wounds covering her naked toes—she doesn't stop dancing. Instead, she gracefully leaps into the air all the while holding up the *stained glass of us*. And she keeps moving...pulling me out of the dark abyss.

As the dancer in the *Opera Show of Us* tugs and pulls me from the nothingness I've become, memories flood back to the surface from that difficult time. And I see all of us blind to Heather's illness. Her hospitalization didn't fix her. It was still there—staring at us.

During her recovery, she moved back into Matt's parent's house. And Mike, Jerry, Sam and I focused on the things we were doing before her hospitalization. And we went forward, full speed ahead.

For me, *Laced* was getting a lot of attention on the national tour. So I focused my time and energy on the reviews that were popping up across the country in newspapers like the Chicago Tribune, the St. Louis Post - Dispatch, and The Kansas City Star. If I wasn't reading a review, I was on the phone with Roland talking about plans for the show and how the cast and crew were holding up on the road. I didn't have a clue how Heather was doing most of the time mentally or physically. And I didn't see her unless she needed money, a prescription refill, food or belongings from her room.

As *Laced* made headlines, Death, by way of eight phone calls, *randomly* played with me and my family. And he did so at his own leisurely pace—usually once per month, but sometimes once every couple of months and sometimes the next day until *almost* a year passed. To do so otherwise would create certainty, and that's the last thing Death wanted. So Heather's suicide attempt was just a tease. Yet again, we had become his victims. But we couldn't get away this time. And while he played with us—his live surplus prey—he was preparing to consume only one of us.

The first call came while I was reading a review. While immersed in the theater critique, I picked up, halfheartedly, and said, "Yeah…" The caller's inability to articulate her thoughts pulled my attention away from the paper. I knew the caller's voice. I had known it for over twenty years. It was Heather. And all I could hear was her sobbing. Troubled by the sound of her voice, I asked her, "Heather! Honey? What's going on?"

"Mom…I have bipolar disorder."

"What? Bipolar dis—"

"Mom…Rita told me I'm bipolar."

"Oh, honey…where are you?"

"I'm on my way home."

"Okay. We'll talk about it when you get here." And with that, we both hung up. I felt horrible. I wasn't with her. And she had yet another diagnosis. Discouraged by the news, I laid the newspaper down on my desk while the question *Now what?* crawled through my mind like a news ticker at the bottom of a television screen.

Later in the day, she told me her psychiatrist added a new medication to her treatment plan. Just like that her doctor remixed her daily cocktail—a mood stabilizer and an anti-anxiety medication—with an antipsychotic. Caught by surprise, again, Mike and I reeled from her newest diagnosis and subsequent medication changes. And life marched on—and Death kept playing with us.

Then, the second call came in, and it pertained to Heather's cosmetology degree. Before the call, her advisor had moved her graduation date from September 2009 to October 2009 due to her hospitalization, so graduation still seemed within reach. But once again, she didn't attend class. As a result, a new advisor, one that had replaced the advisor we spoke to when Heather was in the hospital, called me and requested a meeting.

At the meeting, while looking at Heather, the advisor said, "She seems tired *a lot* when she's here." And then she said, sarcastically, "Do you want me to set up a cot here in the office so you can sleep, Heather?"

Heather didn't reply. Instead, she stared at the floor.

I hated how the advisor talked to her, and I wanted to lash out at her and tell her, "Don't you *ever* talk to my girl like that again!" But, I didn't. Instead, I withheld my anger and looked over at Heather who looked tired and worn down. In that moment, I knew she wouldn't graduate. The meds she was taking were clearly affecting her performance and thus her progress.

The advisor, with little else to say, barked at Heather, "You need to get it together! Just show up on time and get your hours in. It's not hard to do…unless you're an invalid."

Heather looked up at her and then back at the floor. Mike then said, "Heather…Let's go." And he helped her get up from her chair, and they left the room.

I was the last one to leave the room. But before doing so, I looked back at the advisor and said, "You don't know what you're saying, do you? I hope karma's good to you. Oh, and by the way, she won't be back." And just like that, Heather didn't graduate from cosmetology school. She had started off with such drive and ability and had earned eleven hundred out of the fifteen hundred hours required to graduate—but she didn't.

And then, the third call came. Death knew what he was doing. To truly tease me, he would have to mix it up a little by toying with my emotions. One minute, I'd feel extreme sadness and confusion regarding what Heather was going through and the next, I'd feel enormous happiness that pertained to the musical. This awful twist happened when I received a call from Roland who had been keeping me up-to-date on the *Laced* national tour. When my phone rang, and I picked up, I heard someone squealing like a teenage girl who just learned that she made cheerleader tryouts for the first time. To my surprise, when I heard, "Jen?! Are you sitting down?" I realized it was Roland.

I remember laughing at the tone of his voice and saying, "Yeah! What are you doing? Are you drinking?"

"No! Jen! You won't believe it! Uh…"

"The cat got your tongue, Roland? Are you okay?"

"Yes! I'm okay! We're going to Broadway, Jen…the Royal Nobell Theatre to be exact!"

"What?!"

"Yeah! You heard right! Jen?"

With my mouth hanging open, I excitedly laughed and then blurted out, "Yes! I'm here! Oh my God! For real?"

"Yes!" he excitedly yelled while Mike ran into the room to see what I was so excited about.

While holding the phone up to my ear, I looked at Mike and yelled, "Mike! We did it! We made it to Broadway!"

In response, he threw his arms up in the air and yelled, "Yes!" And then he grabbed me and pulled me in close.

As our bodies became one, I lost control of the phone, and it fell to the floor. While caught up in his embrace, I could hear a voice saying, "Jen? Jen? Jen?"

I wiggled out of Mike's arms, picked up the phone and said, "Roland! I'm so sorry!"

He laughed and said, "I'll forgive you this time! I gotta go! I have to make some other calls! I'll call you back again soon! Wahoo hoo! Broadway, Jen! Broadwayyyy!" As his voice faded away, I hung up the phone and looked at Mike in amazement at the news.

Before I could wrap my brain around the mind blowing news, Mike, my parents and I attended the debut of *Laced* on Broadway at the Royal Nobell Theatre. For me, it was surreal. And the flickering lights from camera flashes mixed with the sound of cameras clicking and people cheering us on as we entered the theater oddly soothed the pain and confusion of what Mike and I were experiencing as parents.

After attending the debut of *Laced*, the fourth call came. Death no longer wanted to see me happy and at ease. And his timing couldn't have been more perfect. Mike and I had made arrangements to stay the night in downtown Manhattan that night to celebrate the debut. But before heading to our hotel, we wanted to get something to eat, so we went to Sardi's. While our limo driver drove us to the restaurant, Heather called Mike. And she was frantic. I could hear her through Mike's phone receiver as she yelled and sobbed, "Dad! Dad! I ran over two cats! Oh my God...Daaad!"

"Heather...slow down. Now...what happened?"

Sobbing, Heather said, "I went on a drive, and two cats ran across the road. I hit them both! Dad...only one survived. I picked up the cat that survived with one of my scarves and put it on the passenger seat."

"You shouldn't have touched it!"

"I know...I took it to the animal shelter and put in on the doorstep. Ohhhh, Dad."

Mike comforted her as much as he could by phone. He then called Jerry and Sam to let them know what had happened and asked that they check in on her. By the time he hung up the phone, we were distraught parent's sitting in the back of a limo. Disturbed by Heather's call, we decided that we needed to get back home as quickly as possible. So we directed the limo driver to drive us back to Kensington.

Not long after the call from Heather about the cats, Mike received the fifth call. Again, it was Heather. And just like the call before, she was in tears, and I could hear her sobbing and saying, "Dad..."

"Where are you at?" Mike yelled into the phone receiver.

"Matt's...please...help...tower...fell on my head."

"I'm on my way!" Mike said as he and I ran out of the house to get to her.

When we got to Matt's house, we found Heather inside the house sitting on his parent's staircase. And she was holding the back of her head with her left hand. When we got up close to her, we could see blood dripping from where her hand was. So Mike carefully lifted her hand. And when he did, we both gasped. Underneath her hand was a deep, bloody gash. When we saw it, Mike got a towel and covered it, and I called 911.

While we waited for the ambulance to arrive, she told us that Matt was at work, and she wanted to use his home gym. He had an exercise machine with a lat pull-down bar she wanted to start with. But when she sat down on the bench seat, and pulled the bar down, the cable to the lat tower broke. And the bar, with the force of the weight she was using, fell and hit her on the head. She said the blow to her head caused her to pass out. And she didn't know how long she had been unconscious. By the time the ordeal was over, she walked away from the hospital with twelve stitches in her head. And Death laughed at us knowing this was only practice for what was to come.

The anticipation we *might* receive a call from Heather that something awful had happened became torturous. Mike and I were losing our mental stamina as if we were standing on the edge of a coastal bluff made up of a mixture of moist dirt and loose and crumbly rock. With each phone call from Heather, the dirt and rocks beneath our feet splintered and caved as the erosion of *certainty* slowly gave way to the sea of the unknown.

As Mike and I grappled with call after call, the sixth call came in. When the phone rang, Mike and I were in bed. And again, it was Mike's phone that rang. This time, it wasn't Heather calling. It was Matt. And I could hear him saying, "Mr. Stein! I'm on my way to the hospital with Heather. She got burned from a bottle that exploded!"

"How bad?"

"It's pretty bad, Mr. Stein. We were sitting around a bonfire…and uh—"

"All right…we're on our way." Not knowing how bad the burn was, Mike and I jumped up, got dressed, woke Sam up, ran to the Jeep and raced to the hospital. When we got there, and walked into the outpatient waiting room, we saw Heather sitting next to Matt who had his arm around her. And she was resting her right arm on a pillow. When she saw us, she lifted her head up off of Matt's shoulder and then grimaced in pain. She then laid her head back down on his shoulder and didn't say a word. So Mike asked her, "What happened?"

Before she could respond, Matt said, "She was standing next to the bonfire with my brother, Mitch. He was goofing off and threw a bottle of beer into the fire. And the next thing ya know…boom! The bottle exploded and sprayed her with hot beer! Her right bicep looks meaner than mine now!" he laughed.

We didn't share in his amusement. After his story, we told Heather we loved her and to keep us up-to-date. And then we left. And she walked away from the hospital with a second-degree burn on her right bicep.

And then, the seventh call came while Mike, Jerry, Gabby and I were in Oklahoma visiting my parents. This time, Heather called me. She said, "Matt broke up with me. I'm losing control, Mom. When are you coming back?"

I said, "We'll be back in a few days. It'll go fast. You'll see. And you'll be okay." But deep down, I was sad and depressed—not just for her but for all of us. After Heather and I hung up, I called Sam, who stayed behind, and asked her if she would check in on Heather and make sure everything was okay. Because of Heather's deteriorating mental state, we only spent one day with my parents and then headed back to New York as fast as we could get there.

When we got home, and walked in the house, the house was empty. But within seconds of walking inside, my phone rang. It was the eighth call. And it was Heather calling to say she was moving out of Matt's parent's house because they had kicked her out. And she wanted to know if she could move back in with us. Knowing she was a wreck, I said, "Yes."

During this time, she didn't work. And she talked about stopping therapy because she didn't like her therapist. And she started going over to our neighbor's house because they had a live-in friend she reconnected with.

Mike warned her not to hang out with the guy because he was an unemployed high school drop-out, a drop-out who loved his drugs and who had been charged with assaulting his father and kicked out of his own house because of his violent nature. And he was also three years younger than Heather. But none of that mattered to her.

Instead of listening to Mike's concerns, she started spending her nights with the guy. And she took to his dog, a white, blue-eyed American Eskimo puppy named Snowball. And thereafter, when she would come home, she'd bring the dog with her. And sadly, her appearance got worse. What stood out to me were her feet. They were filthy. It looked like she had been walking barefoot outside. Besides her dirty appearance, she was distant from all of us. When in her presence, she was withdrawn and didn't talk. It's as if we weren't there. She'd walk into the house with Snowball, climb into her bed with the dog and sleep.

And if she was gone for any period of time, when I'd call her and ask about her whereabouts, she'd say, "I'm at a friend's house." If I pried for more details, she'd say, "I'm on the back roads." And when I'd question her about the *back roads*, she wouldn't reply.

Her behavior was getting stranger by the day, so I typed up a timeline to show her counselor. I noted: taking meds as instructed, tired, quit school, impulsive behavior, accident prone, broke up with boyfriend, back at home, poor hygiene, withdrawn, new relationship with next door neighbor, sex?

And then...the calls stopped. Death was done playing. It was showtime.

THE UNWELCOME GUEST

The playing has ceased. The ballet dancer, who's carried the *stained glass of us* along, stops singing and dancing. She drops to her knees on the old oak stage floor and buries her head within her hands.

Now all that remains on the stage is a meek dancer who looks like an insignificant crumpled up discarded tissue paper flower who now cowers in the presence of what was. As she shrinks back in fear, the stage lights flicker on and off, and then they brighten so bright the dancer can't hide her shivering body. And then, the lights go out. And the frightened dancer disappears under the veil of darkness that has blanketed the stage.

With nothing standing between me and a memory that has cruelly toyed with my mental health for years, I see Heather. It's Monday, and she's walking into the house after spending the night at the neighbor's house, again. And I'm talking to her as she closes the door. I'm saying, "I'm concerned about you. I really think you should make an appointment with Rita."

"Mom! I don't like her! I don't want to see her again!"

"Well…there is another option. The social worker at the hospital told me about a counselor who's sought after."

"Oh yeah? Who?"

"Her name is Daria Daxen. Will you at least think about it?"

"Yeah…I'll go."

"Oh! Okay. I have her number. I'll call her now. Let's get you scheduled."

Surprised that Heather didn't mince words, and concerned that she'd change her mind and head back over to the neighbor's house, I called Ms. Daxen's office. When I asked the receptionist who answered my call if Ms. Daxen was taking new patients, she said, "Yes. It's your lucky day! The caller before you canceled his appointment. It's tomorrow though. Do you still want it?"

I took full advantage of the opportunity and said, "Yes! We'll take it."

After collecting the information she needed, she said, "All right. Make sure Heather is here fifteen minutes early to fill out paperwork. See ya tomorrow."

I said, "Okay! Thank you! I'll make sure she's there." And we both hung up.

The following day, Tuesday, May 18, 2010, Heather met with Ms. Daxen at 2:00 p.m. Later in the day, when I saw her at the house again, I asked her how it went. She gave me a thumbs up and said, "I felt comfortable with her."

I didn't respond. I couldn't believe she finally found a counselor she liked. As she turned and walked away from me, she tossed a white appointment card toward the kitchen counter. It caught my attention as it flew through the air. And when it landed on the brown granite surface, I couldn't help but look at it. As I studied it, I noticed that in the center, at the top of the card, was a hand-painted picture of an amethyst-colored flower with the name Daria Daxen, MA, LMHC printed below it. And handwritten in green ink below Ms. Daxen's name was the date 5/25 and the time 1:00 p.m. I was pleased to see that Heather had scheduled another appointment with Ms. Daxen. But after zeroing in on the date and time, my eyes wandered back to the flower. I marveled at it and yelled,

"Hey! Heather! Do you know what type of flower this is on the appointment card?"

From another room in the house, she yelled, "No!"

"It was Grandmama's *favorite* flower! It's a Viscaria flower, a flower that symbolizes a dance proposal! So…if someone gives you a Viscaria flower, they're asking you for a dance!"

Heather didn't respond to my enthusiastic comment. Instead, all I heard was the front door close behind her as she went back over to the neighbor's house. There I stood, alone, not knowing that Death, by way of the appointment card, was inviting me to dance a dance I'd never danced before. And unbeknownst to anyone, except the sender of the appointment card, Heather wouldn't make that appointment.

The same week that Heather saw Ms. Daxen for the first time, I was busy preparing for my first ever interview on the Worth the Interrupt talk show, an interview scheduled for that Friday. And as Heather and I crossed paths that week at the house, I didn't have a clue what was coming my way. All I knew was that Heather finally had a counselor she liked. And I had an interview to focus on, an interview on my favorite American talk show. And it was surreal.

It was also surreal how the evening unfolded the night before the interview. Shortly after Mike, Jerry and Sam showed up at the house, Heather did as well with Snowball in tow. And even though in the back of my mind I knew it was strange that Heather was home, and not next door, I didn't let it worry me. I figured that she wanted to be a part of the intimate celebration we were having at the house before my TV debut.

After our celebratory dinner, we convened in the living room. And the atmosphere was light and full of positivity— even though Heather stayed in the background. After briefly recapping the events that would take place the next day at the TV studio, Jerry dismissed himself and headed home. Sam also dismissed herself and went to her room. And Heather sat down on the couch. When she sat down, she directed Snowball to jump up on her lap. Snowball did as she directed. With Heather present, Mike and I sat down as well and talked small talk. Several times, Mike and I invited Heather into the conversation, but she remained quiet and out of touch. Instead of being concerned, I was happy to have her with us. I didn't question how different her presence was.

At one point, while Mike and I busily chattered about what was happening with *Laced*, Heather said, "Goodnight," and she went downstairs. After she dismissed herself, we went to bed too. But—before I headed to bed, I went downstairs to check on her.

When I got to her room, all I could see was her tousled brown hair sticking out from beneath her pink comforter. And I could hear her crying. Next to her was Snowball lying on top of the thick bed covering. As I approached Heather's bedside, the dog looked up at me and then laid her ears back. Rather than pet the dog, I ignored her, turned my attention toward Heather and tugged at the corner of the comforter. As I tugged, I glanced back over at Snowball who was still looking at me. When my eyes met her blue puppy eyes, she wrinkled her furry white forehead and whimpered. Noticing what looked like concern in the dog's expression, I quickly turned my attention back towards Heather and said, "What's wrong, sweetie?"

Rather than answer me, she continued to cry. Seconds later, from beneath the blanket, she said, "I love you, Mom."

I said, "I love you too! I'm so sorry. Can I do anything?"

"No."

"Okay…I'll be upstairs if you need me."

She replied, quietly, "Okay."

And I kissed her on top of her head and walked away. As I walked out of her room, I noticed three plastic amber vials of medication sitting haphazardly on top of her dresser. Without another thought, I kept walking and went upstairs. And then, after changing clothes, I climbed into my bed and went to sleep.

As I sit here now—with my heart unconsciously beating—I'm reminded that life happens around me with the same ease that my heart beats. And happen it did the night before my big TV interview. Life, as I would know it, was extinguishing right in front of me the night I kissed Heather on the head and exited her room. And as it slowly ceased to burn, I couldn't see it was vanishing before my ignorant eyes.

The next morning, Friday, May 21, 2010, Heather had an eight o'clock appointment to go to that I had forgotten about. It was an appointment she had scheduled for Snowball. I was so focused on preparing for the Worth the Interrupt interview that Heather's vet appointment slipped my mind. When I woke up and saw 7:20 a.m. on my alarm clock, I sat up. As I did, I remembered in that moment that Heather had an appointment, and I also remembered that Heather forgets her appointments, so I jumped out of bed. As my bare-feet touched the carpet, my first thought was *Oh no! Heather's going to miss her appointment!* I then ran down two flights of stairs not realizing I was running through the last corridor of our life as I knew it.

When I got to the basement door, a door that was closed and that was the only barrier between me and the psychological hell hole I was about to fall into, I didn't hesitate to open it. Instead, with all the good motherly intentions I had to help my daughter, I gravitated towards the door, grabbed the doorknob with my right hand, cranked it to the right and opened the entryway to mental hell. When I opened the door, I didn't let go of the doorknob. Instead, when I pushed the door open, I looked down. And when I did, I saw that Snowball had pooped and peed. The tan ceramic tile floor in the downstairs entryway was wet with urine and dog feces, and it smelled horrendous. Since I had been rushing to get to Heather, I had to stop myself from moving forward as the door opened to avoid running through the mess. With the doorknob in my right hand, I grabbed hold of the doorframe with my left hand, to slow the weight of my body from going any further. And when I did, I noticed that Snowball was hiding underneath a side-table to the right. And she was trembling.

I remember looking over at the dog and seeing her ears laid back and her tail tucked up under her backside. As my brain absorbed her strange posture, I noticed that her head was down as if she had gotten into trouble. And even though her head was down, she was looking up at me with her big blue puppy eyes. Her canine behavior seemed odd in that moment. It looked like she was sad, like a human. And then...it hit me. I knew something was terribly wrong. In that instant, I turned my gaze away from the dog, jumped over the dog's foul smelling excretions and ran towards Heather's room all the while yelling, "Heather! Heather!"

When I ran into her room, I saw that her bed was empty. The comforter I had seen her buried under the night before laid abandoned and crumpled up next to her pillow. As I stared in bewilderment at her vacant bed, my peripheral vision on my left side detected movement. I spun toward the movement. And there she was, lying on the floor, with only a gray t-shirt on, and she was moving. But her movements were unnatural. Clueless that something was wrong, I demanded that she speak. I said, "Heather! Heather! What are you doing? Heather! Wake up!"

While I demanded an answer from her, I noticed that her hands and legs were rigid. And her small body was riddled with bruises. I also noticed that she had partially dried white foam around the edges of her mouth. And then...as her body involuntarily convulsed and jerked around rapidly...the cogs in my brain *finally* slipped into place. She was having a seizure. While the reality of what was happening *punched* me in the face, each moment in time I noticed something new, she was uncontrollably hitting her head on a nearby nightstand as her body writhed around. When the reality that my girl was seizing sunk in, I yelled and cried, "Oh my God! Oh my God! Mike! Mike! Help!" With no time to lose, I left her, ran to the next room, grabbed the dog by the collar and ran upstairs screaming, "MIKE!"

Despite my cry for help, Mike and Sam continued to sleep. But I kept screaming, "Something's wrong with Heather! I think she's having a seizure! HELP!" And somehow, while screaming for help, I put the dog outside, grabbed a roll of paper towels and ran back downstairs. By the time I returned to the entryway in the basement, I could hear Mike's voice coming from Heather's bedroom.

While I haphazardly cleaned up the dog mess with paper towels I had ripped from the roll, I could hear him saying, from the other room, "Heather…Heather…Wake up." After picking up what excrement I could, I ran back into her room. And there, free from the whirlwind of chaos I was experiencing, was Mike sitting on the floor next to her. He didn't have time to grab a robe, so he sat next to her in just his underwear calmly saying, "Heather…Heather…Come on…What's wrong?"

I could tell that he was still waking up. With precious seconds slipping by, I grabbed the cordless house phone from the downstairs living room and dialed 911. By the time the dispatcher answered my call and said, "911," Mike was fully awake.

I tried to hold it together the best I could, and in the steadiest voice I could muster, I said, "My name is Jennifer Stein. I live in upper Kensington. I think my daughter is having a seizure. She takes medication for bipolar disorder—"

The dispatcher interrupted me and said, "What kind of medication?"

I didn't respond. Instead, I ran around Heather's room looking for the pill bottles I saw on her dresser the night before. But I couldn't find them. I then said to the dispatcher, "Oh my God! No! I think she overdosed!"

The dispatcher said, "An ambulance is on the way. I need to know what medications she takes."

As I told the dispatcher what meds Heather was taking, while holding my phone between my left ear and left shoulder, I simultaneously pulled open Heather's nightstand drawer. When I did, I saw a pile of loose feathers. Before I could process what I had found, I brushed the feathers to the side. And as I did, I knew in that moment she had taken her pills. I frantically yelled into the phone, "She overdosed! I just found her pill bottles!"

The empty pill bottles were lying underneath the pile of feathers. Next to the feathers was an object she called her *sanctuary*, a small two inch by two inch unpainted wooden box with a window lid that she said reminded her of a pool. And attached to the sides of the box were the remains of fluffy brown and white feathers she had glued on while in the hospital the first time and that she had ripped off the night before I found her. For reasons I'll never understand, she had *destroyed* her sanctuary.

It seemed to take forever for the ambulance to arrive. Knowing the emergency crew would need quick access to Heather, I ran upstairs, glued to the phone still, opened the front door and ran back downstairs. And while I waited for the emergency crew to arrive, I talked with the dispatcher as I ran back and forth between Heather's room and the bottom of the staircase. When the paramedics got to the house, and I saw them in the doorway, I yelled from the basement, "We're downstairs!"

"All right! We're on our way!" a paramedic said. And before I knew it, three medics rushed downstairs and into Heather's room.

One of the paramedic's kneeled down at her side and tapped on her chest. He then asked Mike, "What's her name?"

"Heather!" Mike replied.

The medic then tapped on her chest again and said, "Heather! Speak to me! Heather! What's going on?" He then tapped on her chest harder and repeated her name, "Heather. Tell me what's going on!"

She tried to talk, but she couldn't. Then...she faintly whispered, with pursed and dried out lips, "Ow...You're hurting me."

Suddenly, the medic who was trying to get her to talk said, "Let's go!" And just like they loaded her onto a stretcher and started their trek up the stairs. As they did, they somehow maintained control of the stretcher with Heather on it as they slid around in the remaining dog pee. It was so sad. I couldn't believe it was happening like that.

While I watched the medics slip around in canine waste, while trying to rescue my girl, I questioned my reality. I blurted out, "What the hell? What is going on? How can this be?" My beautiful daughter *was dying* while strapped to a backboard with an emergency crew rushing her out to an ambulance. And the crew—who was trying to save her—was having an awful time getting her up the stairs because of dog shit and pee!

As the medics ran as fast as they could, with Heather on the stretcher, towards the front door, my beautiful Sam ran downstairs past them and into my arms. Grimacing in emotional turmoil, she looked at me and cried out, "Mom! What's going on?"

I hugged her and told her what Heather had done. After I consoled her, the best I could, I then let go of her, grabbed Heather's phone from her nightstand, grabbed Sam's hand and followed Mike who was following the emergency personnel up the stairs. As we ran up the stairs behind them, Mike turned to me and whispered, "Sam's going to have problems after seeing this."

I nodded at him and said, "I know."

While the emergency crew worked on loading Heather into the back of the ambulance, Sam let go of me and called Jerry. After they loaded Heather into the ambulance, and the last medic jumped into the emergency vehicle, the vehicle took off. Mike, Sam and I jumped into our Jeep and sped off too. There we were following an ambulance that was running hot. We were losing Heather. She was already out of our grip. I hated it! I wanted to be right next to her. But I wasn't. Instead, I was with Mike and Sam, and Mike was yelling into his phone, "Roland! Jen can't make the interview! Heather...Oh God, Roland...She might not make it this time. She tried *again* to kill herself. She's dying."

And then, it fully hit me. Heather was out of reach. Unable to contain myself any longer, I burst out crying and yelled, "MIKE! WE SHOULD BE WITH HER! WE SHOULD BE WITH HER!"

By the time we got to the hospital, Jerry was there. He was in the emergency room waiting area with Gabby by his side. When he saw us run into the ER, he ran up to us and hugged all three of us at once. He then motioned, with a nod of his head, for Sam to go with him and Gabby to the waiting room while Mike and I rushed to be at Heather's side.

The emergency room door attendant seemed to know who we were and opened the automatic doors for us when she saw us. As Mike and I ran through the emergency room doorway and into Heather's ER room, a doctor approached us and said, "We're in contact with Poison Control. We're trying to figure out what to do..."

"Is she going to be okay?" Mike asked.

"We don't have answers yet, sir."

And then…he left the room. There Mike and I were all alone with our girl, a girl in full-blown seizure mode. And not one medical professional seemed to know what to do to help her. Mike and I, separated by Heather's ER bed, turned and looked at each other with eyes full of sadness and fear. If the professionals didn't know how to help Heather, then Mike and I certainly didn't know what to do. And with that knowledge, in that moment, we looked down at our helpless girl.

There we were, standing on opposite sides of Heather's ER bed facing one another with our girl, who was still seizing, between us. It was a sight no parent should ever have to see. The ER staff had strapped Heather's hands and legs, with wide leather cuffs, to the bedrails. And the bruises I saw earlier on her body had multiplied. And the way her body continued to shift around and yank at the cuffs, we could see that she was bruising even more.

As she continued to violently convulse, we grew more and more concerned about her head. But our *concern* meant nothing. So we stood there, silent and alone, watching her thrash around with only one reprieve—the minuscule seconds we spent looking at each other before looking back at her.

Finally, Mike had had enough. He attempted to keep her from hurting herself anymore than she already had by placing his hand between the bedrail and her head. While he stood there, trying to protect her from further damaging her head, a nurse walked in and pushed a clear plastic guard up against Heather's lips and said, "I've got to get this in. We don't want her to bite her tongue!"

In unison, Mike and I nodded and said, "Get it in!"

Despite her best effort, the nurse initially couldn't place the guard in her mouth because Heather was clenching her teeth with all the force she had coursing through her body. The nurse didn't let that stop her though and continued to work at prying open Heather's mouth. And as she did, I blurted out, "She has a tongue ring!"

"Glad you told me that! We've got to get it out!" she said.

With an additional task now at hand, she kept prying until she opened Heather's mouth...and then...somehow...she pulled Heather's jaws apart wide enough to insert her index finger and thumb in Heather's mouth, grab hold of the small silver ball underneath her tongue, unscrew it from the barbell tongue ring and pull the barbell and connector out of her mouth. Just as she pulled her hand out of Heather's mouth, Heather's jaws snapped back together. When we heard her top and bottom teeth hit together, the nurse showed me and Mike the palm of her hand and she said, "Got it!"

To my surprise, both pieces to the tongue ring were in the nurse's hand. But the nurse wasn't done yet. She pried open Heather's jaws again and slipped the mouthpiece into her mouth. Just then, Sam approached us. As she did, she looked over at Heather and then broke out in tears. And then, she vanished. I was so torn. I couldn't comfort Sam or Jerry. All I could do was look at Heather and pray that she'd come out of the seizure. While looking at her, I remember feeling inadequate because I didn't know what the hell to do. My girl desperately needed help, and I couldn't give it to her. I felt a sadness so deep it frightened me. I knew we were watching our songbird die. As our dying songbird lay there, the nurse left the room for a brief time and then came back with Heather's empty pill bottles in her hands, pill bottles that the medics had grabbed as they rushed Heather to the ambulance.

The nurse asked us, "How many pills in the bottles?!"

I said, "Uh...there were...they were just refilled yesterday!"

While I stumbled over my words, the nurse called the pharmacy to verify the date the prescriptions had been filled, and how many pills should be remaining. After she confirmed what I had already told her, she hung up the phone, turned and looked at Mike and me and said, "She took ninety psychotropic pills all at once."

Mike and I stood there with sorrow dripping from our eyes. We couldn't believe what was happening. And it seemed like it was happening in slow motion. We needed the medical professionals to stop what Heather had done to herself and reverse the damage that was occurring to her body. But they couldn't. The chemical processes in Heather's body that were in motion when I found her stayed in motion. We were too late. There was no stopping it.

As Mike and I tried to absorb the magnitude of what was happening to Heather, the doctor came back into the room and asked me, "When do you think she took the pills?"

I said, "Let me look at her phone." And I pulled her phone out of my pocket.

As I thumbed through her phone messages, the doctor said, "Do you know why she'd do this?"

Still looking at her phone, I said, "No! I mean…she's been acting different!"

"What do you mean?"

"Her last text message, to her old boyfriend, was at one a.m."

"That means she probably took the pills around that time."

And just as fast as my conversation with the doctor started, it ended. He walked back out of the room, and I stood next to Heather's bedside with the realization she had taken ninety psychotropic pills all at the same time. That's why poison control didn't have an answer. There wasn't one. For over seven hours, ninety capsules filled with a variety of psychoactive drugs had ravaged her body.

As the thought of what she had done sunk in, an alarm sounded and a flock of nurses and doctors flooded Heather's room. And a male nurse, briskly, escorted Mike and me out of her room. We didn't have time to react. He took us to a small private room and then left. Mike and I didn't know what to do, so we sat down and stared at the floor. Soon after, the nurse returned with Jerry, baby Gabby and Sam. And as Jerry and Sam sat down next to me and Mike, the nurse nervously said, "Her heart is failing. We might be losing her. I'll be back to let you know what's going on." He then turned away from us, walked out of the room and closed the door behind him.

There we were…sitting there…stunned at the events that were unfolding. And all I could do was look at my family who were looking back at me with sad faces. The air felt heavy and thick with sickness. I didn't want to be in that little room with my loved ones. It felt like we were *slowly* suffocating. And yet our beautiful Gabby walked around the tiny room innocent to the enormity of what was happening. The only thing, other than us five and the chairs we sat on, was a cross hanging on the wall. That was it. Death had trapped us in a bereavement room we didn't want to be in as our loved one was dying in a nearby room. With nothing but hope to grasp onto, we waited…and waited…and waited more.

After waiting for what seemed like hours, the same nurse who had taken us to the bereavement room opened the door. And as he did, he said, "She pulled through! She's in an induced coma and still in critical condition, but you can go see her. Come on. Follow me!"

Without hesitation, we followed him, and he took us right to her bedside. There she was, and there we were, crying. We were so thankful that she was alive. But we didn't know what to think because now she was in a coma. After seeing Heather for a short time, Jerry and Sam went back to the waiting room with Gabby while Mike and I stood vigil over Heather's bedside. There was no way that anyone could peel Mike and me away from her.

While we stared in disbelief at our girl, the ER doctor joined us and talked to us about why we were taken away from her earlier. I could see him, out of the corner of my eye, looking at her too. And while all three of us stared at her, he said, "Her heart went into SVT's or what we call supra-ventricular tachycardia. It could have killed her. We had to induce a coma and give her drugs to reverse the tachycardia to get her heart into a normal rhythm."

Still looking at Heather, Mike said, "Thank God it worked!"

The doctor replied, "Don't thank me just yet...It's not over."

With nothing more to say, we stared at her. And as we watched her, Mike wrapped his arm around my shoulder and pulled me as close as he could to his side. There we stood faced with the reality that our girl might die despite medical intervention. God how I wished that the rhythms that the doctor talked about were the musical rhythms of songs Heather had written, not the rhythm of her heart fighting to exist.

There our songbird lay, silenced. Her body was finally resting. She was still. It was such an odd juxtaposition to see Heather laying there, sustained not by herself but by the machines next to her, intubated and breathing with the help of a ventilator. My girl, what happened? How did I not see this coming? She was so frail and so close to Death, Death who was waiting for her with outstretched arms. And with every weak heartbeat, she ran further toward his grip. She was so close to the Death that as I stood there and stared at our new reality, thoughts of denial infiltrated my brain as I mentally repelled what happened. *She can't die like this! This can't be happening!* But it did.

While Heather laid in the ICU unit in a coma, Mike and I kept a watchful eye on her. If we weren't standing by her bedside, we were sitting right next to her. And as we watched over her—time—though it seemed to stand still, raced by and became nothing but a blur those first several hours. And as the seconds turned to minutes, and the minutes turned to hours, our razor focus remained unaffected until later that evening when I felt someone touch me on the shoulder. My focus shifted away from Heather and towards whoever was touching me. In response, I turned to see who it was. And as I did, I realized that it was a nurse. As I focused in on her eyes, wondering what she wanted, she said, "It's seven-thirty. The dayshift nurse left at seven, during shift change. I'm Heather's nurse for the night."

I didn't respond. Instead, I stared at her with a blank expression.

In response, she said, "You need to take care of yourself. You won't be any good to her if you don't. She needs you to be strong."

In agreement, I nodded my head at her. And then Mike said, "Honey, why don't you take a break and make some calls? I'm sure everyone is wondering how she's doing. It's okay. I'm staying here. I'm not going anywhere. When you get back, I'll take a break. Go! Get out of here for a minute."

Not wanting to go, but knowing the nurse and Mike were right, I inhaled deeply and then said, "All right…I'll be right back."

And for the first time in hours, I left the room, but not before kissing Heather on her forehead. After I gave her a kiss, I turned and walked away. After using the bathroom and making a few calls, I returned to Heather's side. Mike then did the same. And when he returned, Heather's nurse was right behind him. I could tell that she was on a mission based on her lack of emotion and conversation with me and Mike. As soon as she could get around Mike, she walked up to Heather's bedside, looked down at the urine drainage bag that had been hanging from the side of Heather's hospital bed frame all day and said, while looking at the bag, "This isn't good. She's barely putting out any urine. By now, this bag should need changed. And her latest blood test results don't look good either. Let's hope her kidneys aren't failing. I'll be right back." And she left the room.

When the nurse walked out of the room, I pulled my phone from my pocket and told Mike that I needed to make a call, and I left the room too. As soon as I got out of earshot, I called my mom. As I listened to her phone ring, and waited for her to answer, I looked down at the dull, lifeless floor beneath my feet and paced back and forth. When she answered, and I heard her voice, I stopped in my tracks and cried into the phone, "They think her kidneys are shutting down, Mom! I think we're losing her! Please come as soon as you can!"

I was in such a state of grief I could barely comprehend what she said next. All I can recall is that she mentioned something about being at a reunion, and then she said, "I don't know how yet, but I'm on my way."

After we hung up, I looked back down at the ugly patient trodden flooring and picked up where I left off with my mournful cadence. This time though, while pacing back and forth and staring at the floor, a feeling deep within my body welled up, one I had never felt before. It ripped through every cell of my body and flooded my mind. I wanted to scream to the universe, a universe that seemed unaware, that we had a problem. But I didn't. Instead, filled with trepidation, I turned toward Heather's room and sprinted toward the unknown.

BEAUTIFUL GIRL

"Mrs. Stein!" the nurse said, as I ran into the room. "Slow down! Heather's not going anywhere. She'll be here for a while...one moment at a time, Mom."

"But...you told us her kidneys are failing!"

"I'm so sorry. I didn't mean to frighten you. We're keeping a very close eye on her. The doctor is hoping that she makes a turn for the better here soon. Things change minute by minute. You really should go home...get something to eat and try to get some sleep."

"What? Are you serious?"

"Jen, she's right. If it makes you feel better, we can come back. We'll get sick if we don't," Mike said.

"But—"

"Jen."

"Only if I can come right back, Mike."

"Of course! I'll bring you right back. Take your time. I'll be out in the hallway."

And just like that, after I kissed Heather on her forehead and said goodbye, Mike took me away from her. I knew I needed to take care of myself, but I felt sick to my stomach as I walked away from her and left the hospital. She was in a coma for God's sake. And I was leaving her. The guilt in my mommy guilt thermometer rose ever higher as we drove away from the hospital, so high it burst into pieces.

With guilt contaminating my mind and body as it spewed from my broken mommy guilt thermometer, I went home as instructed. But I couldn't eat. Heather couldn't eat so how could I? And I couldn't sleep. Eating and sleeping were the last things on my mind. I knew I needed both, but I couldn't make myself do either. All I could do was cry when I laid my head on my pillow for the night. I wasn't capable of doing anything else.

And cry I did as I unwillingly relived what had happened earlier that day. Death had branded my brain with the searing reality of suicide. And as a result, the indelible mark of suicide burned into my brain left me that night with questions that viciously bullied me as I tried to sleep. She was at the hospital alive and in intensive care surrounded by a medical team. But how could I trust the team of experts? How could they save her if I, her very own mother, couldn't? And how could I trust her life to anyone when she had the ultimate power to end it?

Death, who hadn't succeeded just yet since Heather was still alive, enjoyed his mournful dance with my mentality. And dance we did, against my will, until I couldn't take it anymore. The only way I could stop waltzing with Death in my head was to get up and out of bed. And that's just what I did.

Before the break of dawn, I woke Mike up and asked him to take me back to the hospital. He held true to his promise and took me right away. While walking the hospital hallways to get to Heather that second day, I remember that I felt a vague sense of optimism wash over me, and as I did, I said to Mike, "Maybe she'll be breathing on her own and smiling that big beautiful smile of hers, Mike!"

But before I could say another word, he grabbed my hand and stopped me from walking any further down the corridor. I reacted by looking down at the floor. And as I did, he turned me toward him, placed both of his hands on my shoulders and said, "Jen, look at me!"

I did as he said, but I didn't say a word, and I couldn't bring myself to look him in the eye.

In response, he carefully grabbed my chin, lifted it up, looked me in the eyes and said "She's comatose, Jen... comatose." And then he hugged me.

After he gave me a hug, he grabbed my hand, and we walked once again towards Heather's room. And as we did, I ignored what he said. And I secretly clung to that unrealistic but hopeful thought because it helped me walk toward whatever was coming my way.

But Mike was right. When we got to Heather's room, and he pulled the privacy curtain back, there she was, comatose in the same hospital bed she was in when we left her the night before, a bed that existed in a small, cold, sterile room. And she was still hooked up to the mechanical ventilator and several other apparatuses. And attached to her body were the same things: cords, IV lines, a breathing tube, a bite block, catheter tubing, a blood pressure cuff, a pulse oximeter and other devices that served the ultimate purpose of keeping her alive.

And it was sadly bizarre. When we walked up to her bedside, I felt like I was a spectator peering into the world of a poisoned princess, a princess who required round the clock medical attention—instead of a kiss from a prince to wake her up. The care this poisoned princess required became blatantly clear as we watched her sleep those first few minutes after we had arrived. While watching her, and looking for any sign she was doing better, we had to step back after an alarm went off and several hospital personnel ran into the room, tended to the alarm, monitored her condition, connected a new device and replenished her IV fluids.

There we were, again, stuck in a room we didn't want to be in. And while we were there, life was occurring all around us beyond Heather's hospital room, but I couldn't see it. All I could focus on was Heather. And Death loved it. The tunnel vision I developed made it easier for Death to play with me.

While I narrowly focused on Heather, I didn't see that Death had changed our life into a game of chance. Each new experience, regarding Heather's recovery, unfolded like a playing card in a deck. But it wasn't just any deck. It was Death's deck of cards. And we didn't know what card he'd hand us next. As Death dealt each new card, we had new wonderings about Heather's life. For example, would she make a quick recovery and be fine? Or would she be in a vegetative state for the rest of her life? Would she need care around the clock? Would she ever be able to speak again? Death had control of over us and was rifle shuffling the deck we call our life with great speed, and Death shuffled the cards so fast that as they cascaded into place, I no longer had a sense of what was to come. Death was tortuously teaching me I had no control over what was to come regarding Heather's health.

But I fought back. And I didn't have to do it alone. I had an unbeatable arsenal: my husband, my two other children and an ICU nurse. With my songbird lying lifeless—silenced by her very own hands—and the whir of a breathing machine that spoke in her place, I leaned on Mike, Jerry and Sam for strength and support and took the advice of a nurse who gave our family a gentle nudge toward coping with our reality. The direction we received from the nurse came when Jerry and Sam showed up and stood with Mike and I alongside Heather's bed. The nurse raised the bed high enough that all four of us stood face to face with Heather. Then, noticing how depressed and quiet we were, she said, "You can talk to her. It's possible she can hear you."

With a little coaxing from the nurse, Mike and the kids took turns walking up to the head of the bed and talking to her. And while they each took a turn engaging in one-way communication with her, I stepped back and sat down. Given her physical state, I knew I'd have my share of time with her, and I didn't want to keep Mike or her siblings from her. She needed them.

After they took turns talking to her, and stepped back, I stood up and walked around them up to the head of her bed. I stood quietly taking in the sight of her lying motionless. The air felt heavy. There I stood wondering what to say. At first, my mouth wouldn't cooperate. There I was—the totality of a mother—crumbling like a sand castle hit by the rising ocean tide as the waves of fear and reality slapped up against me. The proud accomplishment of raising Heather, and knowing I played a key role as her mother, eroded away and became nothing but mere dust particles unrecognizable and gritty. My reality, like salty sea water washing over a fresh wound, stung me as I realized that I didn't have a clue what to do. Moms always know what to do. It's the maternal instinct! It's natural, right? My maternal instinct seemed to have dissolved away into the ocean of life. I didn't know what to do, and I didn't know what to say. Then, like a capsized ship at sea, I righted myself. And I sang to her. My voice was but a mere whisper. But in that moment, I sang *for* her. No longer could she talk, much less speak. So I tenderly, as a mom would do, took over where she so tragically left off.

It made sense that I sang to Heather since music was, and continues to be, a common thread that binds our little family of five besides the profound love that exists between us. And it all culminated in that moment in the ICU when I started to timidly sing. And it became a lifeline.

The song I sang was *Beautiful Girl:* a song that Mike had wrote for me when he met me and that I sang to my girls when they were babies. As I sang to her, I laid my head gently on hers, kissed her forehead and tried not to cry, but the tears inevitably fell. I breathed in her sweet smell and then gently brushed her hair to the side of her beautiful face, and I wept. I then whispered in her ear, "I love you, Heather. We will get through this. And you'll be okay. We're here for you: Dad, Jerry, Sam and I. I love you my beautiful girl."

By evening, on that second day, Mike, Jerry, Sam and I were growing weary. Mike asked one of Heather's doctor's, who had walked into Heather's room to check on her, if he would prescribe me something for sleep. As Mike pleaded with him, he choked back tears and said, "My wife...she hasn't slept since this happened. Can you please give her something?"

The doctor, without hesitation, said, "What pharmacy do you use?" And he called in a prescription from his personal cell phone.

But later that night, when Mike, Sam and I got back home after a quick stop at the pharmacy, I found myself in my bathroom staring at my reflection in the bathroom mirror. As my reflection, and my surroundings, bounced back at me, I didn't see my face or the opened prescription bottle that lay next to me on the bathroom counter. Instead, I fixated on the reflection of the small white disposable bathroom cup I had pressed up against my bottom lip, a cup that contained the fluid necessary to wash the pink, oblong shaped pill that sat on my tongue down my throat. Despite having in my possession a magic pill that would help me sleep, and that would wash away my anxiety and fear, the cup fell from my hand. As the cup hit the bottom of the marble sink, and the water splashed out, I leaned in toward the mirror, opened my mouth, stuck my tongue out and stared at the pink pill that sat on my tongue. As I stared at the pill, as it absorbed into my flesh, Mike yelled, "Heather! You okay in there?"

And as his words sunk into my ill brain, I spit the pill out of my mouth, and into the palm of my hand, and yelled back, "I'm good," and then dropped the pill in the toilet, flushed it down the porcelain throne and joined Mike in bed. And while he dozed off, I laid in bed with eyes wide open with the image of our poisoned princess lying alone in an ICU unit fighting to take her next breath. And Death grinned.

STAND BY ME

I see her. There she is. There's my girl. And I'm talking to her, "Heather...Heather. What are you doing? Heather! Wake up!" She's not answering me. Wait! Something's wrong. I feel cold. The icy feeling is dragging me away from her...my body's trembling...I'm crying. What the hell? Why am I so cold? I can't get to her now. Damn it! She can't hear me. Wait! Someone's gasping for air. Shit! It's me. And I'm in bed.

As I transition from REM sleep to the reality I live in, I shiver. And I curl up my body into a fetal position and pull the blanket up around my neck. I then look over at my digital alarm clock, a black box the size of a brick with red glowing numbers on the display, and the more I look at the fuzzy numbers, the more I notice that my head feels like a paperweight glued to my pillow. And the rest of my body...it feels like it's warming up, and my brain is waking up as I focus in on the glowing numbers. And then...my eyes pop open. It's 7:20 a.m., the exact time I found Heather a few days before. And tears well up in my tired eyes, then flow down the side of my face and spill from my eyes onto my pillowcase.

The coldness of my wet pillowcase grabs my attention, and so does the sound of Mike's voice as he says, "You had a flash back...didn't you?"

With my attention on Mike now, I don't answer. I can't. The fear and pain I'm feeling makes it difficult to think of anything else.

"I'm so sorry, honey," he says as he lays his head on my head and wraps his arms around me.

Again, I don't answer. Instead, I focus on the warmth of his arms around me and the weight of his head on mine and the wetness of my tears on my pillowcase. And then—in silence—we get up, get dressed and head to the hospital.

And there we were *again* at the same infirmary, an infirmary we wanted no part of. And as we walked the maze like passageways, hand in hand, we walked in silence toward Heather and the continuation of what was *unknown* regarding her mental and physical state. But before we stepped foot in her room, we stopped by the nurses' station. And as we did, Mike perked up and in a hopeful voice asked the nurse on duty, who was sitting at a desk looking at a computer screen, "How's Heather doing?"

The nurse glanced up at Mike and said, "Good morning, Mr. Stein. This morning, the doctor ordered a reduction of the propofol. So I started the reduction in dosage. They're bringing her back from the coma, Mr. Stein."

"Oh! That's fantastic news! We'll finally be able to talk to her!" Mike said.

"Well, I wished it worked like that, Mr. Stein. But it doesn't. Let's hope for the best. Heather has a lot of work ahead of her. We don't know what to expect as she comes out of the coma. Some patients fight the ventilator. Let's hope she doesn't."

"Oh," Mike said.

Already in a weakened state and unable to process the sadness I saw in Mike's eyes, I looked away from him and asked the nurse, "Can we see her now?"

"Of course you can, Mrs. Stein. Just be prepared to leave if needed. I can't tell you what will happen...but there will be a lot of activity in her room today."

With little hope to cling to, I didn't respond to her. Instead, I said, "Come on, Mike. Let's go." And we walked into Heather's room. And again, there she was—the same poisoned princess we had left the night before. And the same machine that sustained her life the night before, housed in ivory-colored plastic, was still there—artificially breathing for her.

As the machine blew oxygenated air into my sleeping girl's lungs through plastic tubing that had been inserted through her mouth and down into her windpipe, I stared at her. And the more I focused on her beautiful round face and her thick and shiny long brown hair, and her tender dark brown eyelashes that fringed her sleeping eyelids, the more I noticed the bite block in her mouth and the plastic tubing that protruded from her mouth that connected to the life-support machine. And then, needing to refocus on something other than the artificiality of what was keeping my girl alive, I asked Mike, "Do you think she'll have any brain damage?"

He whispered, "I don't know, Jen," as the machine took yet another mechanical breath in and then out…

His answer didn't suffice. Desperate to hear something other than the sound of the ventilator control system delivering the mandatory breathing pattern for Heather, I pushed him to say more, and I said, "What do you think she'll be like?"

And again, he whispered, "I don't know, Jen."

Still in need of hearing his voice and not the fake lung's breathing pattern, I asked him, "What about her memory? Will her memory be okay?"

And all I heard in response to my question was the sound of the mechanical ventilator as it switched from inspiration to expiration and back again. And each time it recycled, it reminded me of the sound I make when I jump into a swimming pool, the sound of taking a deep breath in before plugging my nose and diving into the water and then the sound of my breath as I exhale when I come up out of the water.

And while my ears took in sounds I didn't want to hear, Mike wrapped his arm around me and pulled me close. And we both stared at our girl. And we knew only one thing in that moment. Our girl was alive. That's it. Other than that, we had no clue what was to come. And Death continued to smile.

That day, Jerry wasn't with us. After Mike asked the doctor on duty for sleep medication for me the night before, Jerry broke down in tears in Heather's ICU room and left the hospital. After he left, he called me. And I could barely understand him because he was crying so hard. Through his tears, he said, "Mom, I'm so sorry. I can't take seeing Heather like that. I had to leave. I hope you and Dad understand."

I told him, "I do. I love you so much, Jerry! Take care of yourself. Just let Dad and I know how it's going. Please...keep us posted."

"I will, Mom."

"I love you, Jerry."

And he replied, "I love you too, Mom. Bye."

Even though Jerry left the hospital, the second night, Sam stayed and went home with us that night. So on the morning of the third day, she joined Mike and me later that morning at the hospital. And I remember her standing to my left. And even though we didn't talk, her presence next to me was comforting as we stood there in silence, together, watching over Heather. But Death didn't like that I felt comfort. So when Heather opened her eyes for the first time since being put into the coma—all hell broke loose.

As she slowly woke up, and took in her surroundings, she looked around the room with wide-open eyes, eyes that darted back and forth, up and down and then back and forth again. And it was a marvelous moment. It was so marvelous that Mike, Sam and I shouted, in unison, "Yes! She's awake!"

But the smiles that had broken out across our faces vanished as quickly as they appeared as we watched sheer panic wash over Heather's face as she realized that she wasn't breathing on her own. And then, the unthinkable happened. She tried to spit the blue plastic bite block out of her mouth with her tongue and the muscles in her throat. As she worked at getting the bite block out of her mouth, I saw the breathing tube move up and down. When I realized what she was doing, I yelled, "Mike!"

Just then, Sam bolted out of the room, and Mike ran up to Heather's bedside and said, "Heather...calm down...just breathe." While he worked at soothing her, I stood there in total shock.

While I watched the breathing tube bob up and down in Heather's mouth like a buoy off the ocean shoreline, the respiratory nurse said to Heather, "You're on a breathing machine, Heather. We're taking you off of it soon. But in the meantime, I need you to cooperate by relaxing the best you can. You need to let the machine breathe for you!" But Heather didn't listen to her. Instead, she continued to push at the tubing with her throat muscles.

Since Heather wasn't cooperating with the nurse, Mike stepped back in and said, in a gentle but firm voice, "Heather...breathe...just breathe."

When she heard her dad's voice, she calmed down. But then, after a few minutes passed, she worked again at expelling the plastic equipment from her airway. Mike then again repeated to her, "Just breathe..." as he brushed the bangs on her forehead to the side of her face. And before we knew it, a pattern ensued. She would try to expel the bite block and breathing tube, and Mike would try to calm her and tell her to breathe.

While I continued to watch, in shock, as my girl fought the very thing that was keeping her alive, the nurse shouted, "You need to stop fighting it, Heather!" And then she left the room.

After the nurse walked out of the room, Mike said, "I'll be right back. I need a minute." Startled by Mike's announcement, Sam and I turned and looked at each other. Then Sam turned away from me and toward Mike and yelled, "Dad! Don't go! She won't listen to us! She only listens to you! You know that!"

"It'll be okay, Sam. I won't be gone long—"

"Pleasssse stay. She doesn't listen to us, Mike. If you leave, she'll spit out the mouth guard!" I said.

"Jen…I need a minute. I'll be right back. Just give me a minute." As he walked toward the curtain to exit the room, he turned and looked at me one last time and said, "It'll be okay. Just get the nurse if she does it again. I'll be back." And he turned away from me and exited the room.

After he left, Sam and I looked at each other, and then we both turned our gaze toward Heather. And we watched the breathing tube bob up and down and the bite block continue to slip further from her mouth. Then, without warning, Sam yelled, "Stop it, Heather! Stop it! I hate you! Why did you do this to yourself? Do you really want to die?"

I grabbed Sam's arm and yelled, "Sam! You don't mean that!"

And in return, Sam gasped and cried, "Oh my God! Heather. I didn't mean it. I'm so sorry, Heather." And then she slinked back away from Heather's bedside and stood behind me.

And then…just like we feared, the bite block tumbled from Heather's mouth. And it landed on her chest just below her chin. While I watched the blue bite block move up and down as her chest rose and sank in reaction to the breathable air that was moving in and out of her lungs, Sam ran out of the room and got the nurse. And I said to Heather, "It'll going to be okay! Hang in there, sweetie."

Several minutes later, after the nurse returned, reset the bite block, and then she exited the room again, Mike walked back in. And when he did, Sam said, "Dad! She did it! She spit it out!"

"What?" he said.

"We told you, Dad!"

"It's okay, Sam," I said as I redirected Mike and Sam's attention back toward Heather with the nod of my head. And while Sam and I looked at Heather with relief in our eyes, Mike picked up where he left off and encouraged her to let the machine do the breathing for her. And for the rest of the day, she swung, like a clock pendulum, from a state of rest to a state of upheaval and back again.

Watching her transition from the ventilator to breathing on her own was *jarringly* brutal to watch. I can't imagine what she was feeling as she transitioned from the ventilator to breathing on her own. All I knew was that I felt thankful for the person who invented the glorious machine, a machine that seemed like an oddity as it sustained her life and kept her from entering through Death's doorway as if it were a mechanical guardian, clothed in plastic, watching over her—giving her life.

And that day, the glorious mechanical guardian, standing by my girl's hospital bedside, became a symbol, a 3D symbol representing life for the *lingerers*—those who have swung through the doorway of life but who haven't swung near enough towards Death's doorway to enter it. And my beautiful girl happened to be one of those *lingerers* caught in the unattached space between life and Death—who was waiting for her.

But, when it was time for her to breathe on her own, this magnificent breathing machine became her enemy. And she fought it desperately—as if it were a dangerous beast—and she wrestled with it and tried with all her might to remove what had become a painful suffocating object that was keeping her from breathing on her own.

As the day wore on, I was beyond ready for the ICU team to remove the breathing tube. I couldn't take seeing her in such pain and misery any longer. And thank God, the time finally came when the nurse said, "We're going to try to take her off the ventilator. But she has to pass three breathing trials *first* before we can remove the breathing tube."

The thought of Heather having to go through what seemed to be torture was difficult for me to process. It seemed like all of us had already been to hell and back. And now she had to do what?! I braced myself for what was to come. But I worried about her ability to make it through the breathing trials. She was already fighting the ventilator. How could she possibly continue to stay on the machine? Somehow, Heather had to breathe on her own, without the help of the machine and with the breathing tube still in place. It seemed impossible, but we reassured her she could do it. I remember hearing Mike say, "I know, Heather, that you want the tube removed. In order for the nurse to take it out, you need to relax and try to breathe on your own. You can do it! You want this removed!"

Sam also reassured her. She said, "Heather, you can do it!"

And I followed suit and said, "Heather, I know you can do this!"

And, as painful as it was, she did. Once she passed the three breathing trials, the nurse escorted us out of the room. As she did, she whispered, "You can stay, but I don't recommend it. Patients can have a hard time with it. I don't think it's something you want to see."

We did as the nurse recommended and left the room. As we nervously paced back and forth outside of Heather's room, ICU personnel took her off of the ventilator. And soon after, they allowed us to visit her again. After checking in on her, the three of us took a much-needed break. Since we knew she was making progress, we went home to take care of errands, to eat and to rest. And we felt a bit relieved. But it felt like we were still on pins and needles because we didn't know yet the effects of the overdose and subsequent coma. All we knew was that Heather had fought the breathing tube, and she was off of the breathing machine. The state of her mind and body was a mystery.

Even though I didn't know the state of Heather's mind, my own mental state was in shambles. As sick as it was, this is just what Death wanted. And Death sat back and indulged in watching what happened next as if my life had become a TV series marathon—a marathon that was leading to the shattering of the *stained glass of us*.

When Mike and I returned to the hospital later that same day, I remember that I felt agitated the closer we got to Heather's hospital room in the intensive care unit. I could hear nurses talking at the nurses' station. I could hear doctors being paged. I could hear family members talking in the next room. I could hear the telephone ring at the nurses' station. I could hear the squeaky wheels on a laundry cart being pushed by an attendant somewhere in the ICU unit. The external noises bothered me to the point I wanted to yell, "Stop! Just stop! We have a problem here! Can't you see?" But I didn't.

When we finally reached Heather's room, Mike slid the hospital curtain—with what looked like ease—to the right. As the curtain moved along the rail, I winced at the high-pitched sound that rang out as the metal curtain hooks scraped along the metal rail. And as the curtain swung to the right, we stopped in our tracks.

There our girl sat in the hospital bed looking at us while she rocked back and forth with her arms extended straight out, her wrists bent inward, her thumbs tucked under her fingers, her hands tightly clenched into fists and her feet extended forward with the tips of her toes curled down as if her feet were in perfect ballet pointe. As my eyes absorbed her strange posture, my already broken heart broke even more. And I didn't want to accept what I was witnessing. But I had to.

And then to my surprise, as I continued to take in the sight of my girl rocking back and forth, she somehow crossed one arm over the other and brought her tightly clenched fists up toward her chest and she tried to say something. But what she said only came out as a murmur because she couldn't fully open her mouth. And in that moment, I wondered who the girl was that sat in my girl's place.

Odd feelings surfaced in my gut, and questions swirled around in my already dizzy head full of images I hadn't fully processed yet. *My girl! What happened? Where is she?* I didn't know the girl who I was looking at. *Am I in the wrong room? God! Please let me be in the wrong room! I don't want to be here.* And in that moment—like the gravitational pull of a black hole—the realization she was my girl pulled me back into my reality. And new thoughts filled my mind. *Oh, my God! That girl is mine! She needs me!* And I raced to be at her side, and Mike followed. And again, we were standing at her bedside. It didn't matter that she appeared different. She was ours...ours to love and take care of. And so we did.

As I clumsily fell into my newest reality, I was so lost in my own world of sadness, grief and loss I wasn't able to make myself available to my other children. And I was painfully, and acutely, aware that I was of no good to my son and youngest daughter. My lack of availability to Jerry and Sam was yet another sad reality in a world that seemed to have grown painful and confusing.

But it was what it was. Mike and I were in a constant state of emotional adjustment while we supported Heather as she came out of the coma. One moment, we were victorious because she woke up from the coma. The next moment, we were at a loss for words, and indescribably sad, as we watched her attempt to eject the breathing tube from her airway.

And then once over that hurdle, we found ourselves in a state of sadness again as we watched her move in an alien like contorted fashion the more she came out of the coma. And later that same day, when Sam came back to the hospital, Heather pulled out her urinary catheter.

Naturally, Mike and I had great difficulty seeing our daughter physically and mentally altered. We'd take turns and one by one leave the room for a short time. I remember Mike crying at one point as he left. We truly had no idea what was to come. It seemed that Heather had damaged herself to the point of being almost unrecognizable as she moved backward and forward unintentionally and murmured words we couldn't understand. But, as the evening wore on, Heather became calmer and more relaxed. Even the contorted movements she made slowly ceased. Also, her speech changed. Her murmuring turned into actual words we could comprehend. However, there was a catch. Despite the miraculous changes we watched occur, her memory seemed to be impaired. She didn't know where she was or why she was there. Also, what she said made little sense.

Hour by hour, her memory improved, and we were able to understand her. And we had the privilege of witnessing her beautiful yet fragile personality come back to life. Around this time, my parents showed up from out of town. I remember when they walked into Heather's hospital room in the ICU. They hesitantly walked up to Heather's hospital bed and then conversed with her.

She was beginning the process of eating solid food again and was enjoying her first taste of hospital ice-cream. When she saw my parents, she stopped eating and smiled at them. Her grandparent's, without knowing it, got to see her smile for the first time since she had tried to end her life. In response to Heather's smile, my mom said, "I don't know about that ice-cream! Does it taste good, Heather?"

Heather, laughing as loud as her weak body would let her, said, "Grandma! It beats your tomato soup you made me eat when I was nine!"

We all burst out laughing. Heather appeared to have returned to us in one piece. Her voice was still fragile, but she had her voice back. At that point, it seemed, we had our Heather back the way we remembered her. What a miracle it was.

Since Heather was doing better, the three of us took my parent's out to dinner. After dinner, out in the parking lot, I told my mom, "Why don't you and Dad head to our house. Sam has her own car so you can follow her. She'll help you get your suitcases inside, and you can get set up for the night in the guest room. Mike and I want to go back to the hospital and see Heather before we head home for the night."

My mom replied, "That sounds good, honey. Tell Heather we love her, and we'll see you after a bit."

"Okay. I love you, Mom. And thank you for being here!"

"Jen...I wouldn't have it any other way."

My mom and I hugged and said, "I love you!" at the same time and then temporarily parted ways.

Later that night, once back at home, Mike, Sam and myself sat in the living room with my parents. The three of us sat together on a large sofa across from my parents' who sat on a mid-size loveseat. None of us talked much. It felt awkward. I had gotten used to the hospital atmosphere, an atmosphere where we as a family experienced continuous activity around us yet we were oddly disconnected from what was occurring around us. We sat in the hospital for days alone in our thoughts. No one knew us there. We didn't have to connect with anyone, other than Heather's medical team, and honestly, I didn't want to connect with anyone. And I didn't understand why.

And for the first time in my life, I felt a divide between my mom and myself as if I was on the edge of a cliff at the Grand Canyon with red layered bands of bedrock beneath my feet miles away from my mom who was opposite of me on the other side of the massive chasm. I could see her, and she could see me, but I didn't know how to reach her to tell her I had an injury and that my husband and kids had an injury too brought on by what Heather had done to herself, and I didn't know how to tell her I didn't know what to do. I knew that the separation I felt wasn't my mom's fault. She had nothing to do with what Heather had done, but an emotional and intellectual separation between my mom and I undeniably existed. While I silently looked at my mom with eyes begging for help, she said, with love in her voice, "You'll find a place to put it, Jen."

I nodded in response to her comment and clung to what she told me. She threw me a lifeline from across the gargantuan chasm that separated us, and I grabbed hold. I clung to those seven words and internally repeated them to myself cementing them in my brain in what had become a chain of desolate interlinking neurons. *You'll find a place to put it... You'll find a place to put it...*

Little did any of us know, while we sat in the living room bogged down by feelings of awkwardness, Jerry had showed up and was sitting in his car outside of the house. Right after I nodded at my mom, I heard the front door open. As we sat in the living room, looking like wilted florist flowers after a week, I said, "Hello?"

In response, we all heard a deep voice from the entry way say, "Oh! Hi, Mom!"

Even though Jerry was out of sight, I knew it was him, and I yelled, "Jerry! I'm so glad you came over! Grandma and Grandpa are here!"

He didn't respond.

We then heard him walk up the stairs to the living room. When he came into view, he looked like I felt. And without saying anything to any of us, he walked up to me. I stood up from the sofa I was sitting on to give him a hug. But before I could reach out to him, he wrapped a beautiful hand crocheted magenta colored prayer shawl around my shoulders and said, "Mom...when I left the hospital last night, I drove over to the church down the street from the hospital. I don't know why, but I did. And while I was there, praying, an elderly woman joined me in prayer, and then she gave me this scarf. When she put it in my hands, she said the church congregation had prayed over it for peace and healing. And then she told me to take it to the person who needs it."

Awestruck by Jerry's gift, I didn't say a word. But the silence didn't last because someone in the living room started crying. To this day, I'm still not sure who it was. But I think it was Sam. With the prayer shawl lovingly wrapped around my shoulders, I gasped and cried as well and embraced Jerry tightly saying, "Jerry...Thank you. You have no idea how much this means. I love you, sweetie." What a beautiful gesture it was. I felt feelings of joy and thankfulness well up within my tired soul, and I felt a bit revived for the days ahead.

The following morning, during our drive back to the hospital, Mike asked me, "So what time do you think your parents' will head to the hospital?"

I replied, "They're gone."

"What? They're gone?" Mike said.

"Mom told me last night, before we went to bed that since Heather was doing better, her and Dad were going to head back to the reunion. I don't think they understand. I don't get it."

"I don't get it either, Jen. Let's not talk about it. Heather needs us. That's what matters."

Silence filled the atmosphere in the Jeep, and I felt sick that my mom had left us. My mind filled with questions. *How can she do this? I need her...Heather needs her, Sam needs her, Jerry needs her, we all need her. Where's my mom? Mom?!*

FALL RISK

I'm back at the hospital with Mike by my side, and a nurse is saying, "Heather's being moved to the seventh floor today."

The agitation I felt the day before crawled back to the surface of my skin. And I yelled at her, "No! I think you got it wrong! You must be in the wrong room! Our daughter's *still* recovering! Can't you see? She's still drowsy from the meds she received in ICU and weak from the drug overdose and coma! Moving her would be ludicrous!"

"Jen! Stop it!" Mike said as Sam, who had arrived at the hospital shortly after us, walked into the room.

I ignored him, and Sam, and instead pointed with my index finger at Heather and yelled, "Look at her! I want you to *look* at her!"

The nurse looked at Heather. And I know she saw the same thing as me and anyone else in the room at that moment. She saw, lying in the ICU bed, a small, pale, weak young lady with a willowy body covered in dark purple bruises, bruises that were the physical evidence of the jolting seizures she had experienced in her bedroom the night before I found her. And the young lady we were all looking at had bruises on her wrists and ankles from the leather cuffs that were used to keep her tied to the emergency room hospital bed while she seized. And she had a large bruise above her left eye where she had hit her head on her bedroom nightstand during the seizure at the house. There was no way the young lady we all were looking at was strong enough to be moved upstairs.

After looking at Heather, the nurse looked at me and said, "Mrs. Ste—"

I didn't let her finish. Instead, I yelled, "Can't you see she's just now recovering? Could you have a *little* sympathy? My God! She doesn't want to be here! Why are you making this more difficult than it is? Are you *sure* you have the right patient?!"

Before I could utter another word, Mike yelled, "Stop it!" and he grabbed me by the arm and pulled me away from the nurse.

But I yanked my arm from his grip, walked up to the nurse and then broke down into a puddle of tears. And through my tears, I said, "I know you've been through this before. But we haven't. That's *my* girl…Her *name* is Heather. I want you to treat her as if she's your own. What the hell's wrong with our mental health care system? She's human! Can't you see—she's human. Don't treat her like you treat everyone else. My girl isn't a robot. She has feelings, and she has a brain that comprehends *everything* that is going on with and around her. And she has a heart. Yes! It beats like everyone else's. But it's hers. It's *her* heart. What is she to you? Huh? Tell me?"

I could hear Sam crying, and then she yelled, "Mom! Stop it!"

Like a runaway train, I couldn't. I pointed my finger at Mike who had his arms wrapped around Sam. And I said, "Look at my family! Look!" And even though I saw that Sam was crying, I continued to yell. And I pointed back at Heather and said, "All she is to you is just another patient moved along the conveyor belt of our healthcare system from ambulance to an emergency room to ICU and from ICU to the seventh floor. And from there, she's sent back home *still* bruised and weak and mentally fragile! What the hell?"

From the doorway, a female voice interrupted me and said, "Is this Heather Stein's room?"

The nurse who I had been yelling at turned away from me and toward the doorway and said, "Yes. This is Heather Stein's room. Come on in."

The young lady did as the nurse said and sat down on a chair next to Heather's bedside. As she sat down, the nurse said to her, "I want *you* to treat her as you would want treated yourself." And then the nurse looked back at me and said, "This is Janis. She's a patient safety assistant. She'll be here to help Heather get out of bed to use the bathroom, and she'll sit with her until they have a bed upstairs. And Mrs. Stein...I can't imagine what you're going through. Just know I'm here for you and your family. And don't stop yelling...okay?"

I nodded at her. And then she gave me a hug and walked out of the room. I knew Janis was there to make sure that Heather didn't hurt herself. But I felt uneasy about it because I knew what was coming. No matter how much I yelled and cried—my girl was going upstairs.

Even though I knew Heather was in need of continued medical care, and psychotherapy, the transition wasn't easy. My mind was fraught with anxiety because I knew Heather would be out of reach—again. And this time, it felt like she was going away to a prison.

Regardless, the time came. And a nurse from upstairs walked into Heather's room after dinner. She sat down next to Heather and had "the talk" with her. While she spoke with Heather, Mike looked at me and said, "*Don't* say a word. She'll be okay." I listened to him and refrained from unleashing my frustrations out on the newest nurse who had come into our lives.

From Heather's visual perspective, Janis was sitting on a chair in the background by the bathroom on Heather's left side. And Mike and Sam stood to the right of her hospital bed while I stood to her left. And the nurse from upstairs sat at the foot of her bed. And from the seated position she was in she leaned in towards Heather and told her she had two options. "You can either sign the **Application for Voluntary Admission** and go upstairs to the behavioral health unit *or* go to the *state* mental health center."

Heather said, "I don't want to go back upstairs."

The nurse said, "You *don't* want to go to the state hospital." For several minutes, Heather and the nurse went back and forth. Finally, the nurse said, "If you don't comply, the hospital staff will have to restrain you and take you to the state hospital. You're going upstairs—or to the state hospital—because you tried to kill yourself. You're a harm to yourself. You *have* no choice."

Heather didn't say a word in response and relented. She then reluctantly signed the document. But that wasn't the end. When the nurse got up to leave the room, she said to Heather, "You have one more task. A guard will need to frisk you. We have to make sure you have nothing on you that you could use to harm yourself."

Heather, with concern in her eyes, looked at me and then at the nurse but didn't say a word. And I kept my mouth shut. But it bewildered me that a guard had to run his or her hands up and down a patient, dressed in a hospital gown, in search of a hidden weapon. Heather had nothing on her she could use to hurt herself. She was struggling with the fact that she wouldn't be leaving the hospital. The added blow that a guard had to pat her down added to an already difficult situation.

When the time came for her to be moved upstairs, a guard walked into her room. But the guard wasn't who we expected. The guard was a male guard. When I made eye contact with him, Mike walked over to where I was standing and placed his hand on my shoulder. In response to the pressure of his hand on my shoulder, I looked at him and said, "Why couldn't a female guard have patted her down?"

In return, he said, "I don't know, Jen. Let's hope this all ends soon. I can't take much more either. Let's be strong for Heather."

And so it happened. The guard frisked Heather while her family watched. There she was—a fragile, pale, willowy thin and bruised young lady shaky from attempting to end her life and the consequences thereafter—being treated like a criminal. I shook my head in disbelief and muttered, "There has to be a better way."

After the guard patted her down, a hospital attendant took her upstairs by wheelchair. And we followed. It was an odd yet beautiful juxtaposition as we followed our loved one as if we were geese dropping out of the sky to attend to a wounded gosling. And though I was mad minutes before, I felt grateful that the hospital staff allowed us to go with her to her room even if it was only for a short time. There we were following an attendant who was pushing a wheelchair, a wheelchair with Heather sitting in it, down the hospital hallway toward an elevator.

When we got to the elevator doors, and they opened, we squeezed into a four-person elevator with the attendant and Heather positioned in front of us. And as the elevator churned its way up the elevator shaft, we quietly stood there knowing soon she'd be out of reach. And then the elevator stopped, and the doors effortlessly opened. The hospital attendant, carefree, pushed Heather's wheelchair out of the elevator and down the hallway to the entranceway of the behavioral health unit.

The pain of seeing Heather, yet again, go through the doors—after a nurse from behind a glass window pushed the unlock button—was unspeakable. That's all it took. The nurse pushed the button. And we heard, *CLICK...BUZZZZ.* And then two large doors swung open and swallowed our loved one up. Then, the nurse nodded to us—giving us the okay to follow Heather. With the nurse's head nod, we quickened our pace and followed right behind the hospital attendant and Heather. And as we did, I saw the bold red line that ran from one side of the hallway to the other. I hated it. I didn't want to see that red line again. It was physical evidence *again* of the fact that my daughter was sick—mentally sick.

Regardless of how much I hated that red line, we crossed it, and then the assistant turned the wheelchair to the left and then pushed the wheelchair into a large vacant room. The room looked dismal, and it was cold. There were two beds in the room, and there was a small bathroom. The attendant pushed the wheelchair up to the bed farthest away from the door and nearest to the window. He then assisted Heather as she transferred herself from the wheelchair to the bed, and then he left the room as quick as he had entered it. And there we stood—a shell of a family—with Jerry still missing.

While Heather laid there in the hospital bed, looking like a delicate human paper doll that a simple breeze could pick up and steal away from us, we walked around the room and made small talk. After checking out the bathroom, Sam returned to Heather's bedside and said, jokingly, "Hey! You'll have to check out the bathroom. The tile's okay...I mean, it is a little outdated...but the patterns nice!" Heather—looking exhausted and weary from the suicide attempt, the ambulance experience, the trauma in the ER, the coma and the difficult and laboring work of coming off the breathing machine, the loss and then the return of her memory and the sheer physical toll that her body had endured—smiled.

Not long after the nurse assistant left the room, Heather said, "I have to use the bathroom."

Sam reached for Heather's arm to help her up from the bed, but Heather said, "I got it." And she got up from the bed. As she walked away from us, she faltered so I ran up to her, grabbed her arm and helped her get to the bathroom door.

THE LUGGAGE DROP

Once there, she said, "I got it, Mom." And she walked into the bathroom and closed the door.

As the door shut, I turned to Mike and said, "This isn't right! She could fall!"

Mike nodded in agreement and as soon as he saw a nurse walk by Heather's room he got her attention and said, "Hey! Our daughter is stumbling when she walks. Can we do something about this? Do you have a *fall risk* bracelet we can put on her?"

The nurse, standing out in the hallway, said, "Sure. I'll be right back." And she walked away and returned shortly after with a bright yellow plastic bracelet with the words **FALL RISK** printed in bold black letters on it. After we helped Heather get back to her hospital bed, the nurse placed the bracelet on Heather's left wrist and then left. And we felt *some* relief knowing at least Heather had a bracelet on to warn the hospital staff she was a fall risk. But we were uncomfortable that we had to *ask* for the bracelet. Left to fend for herself, she could have gotten seriously injured. With that in mind, it was difficult for us to leave her that night. But we did. And before I knew it, I was back at home in my bed with Mike by my side. And we were miles from my girl who was lying in a hospital bed—in a cold room, in a gigantic hospital, medicated and bruised after trying to killing herself—all alone.

I tossed and turned as I tried to get some shut-eye. But the tossing and turning didn't work, so I jumped up from my bed, got my robe on and ran to my office. And in the dark, without a single light on, I hit the power button on the computer, entered my password and then sat down on my office chair and waited for the home screen to pop up. As soon as I saw the computer desktop, I clicked on the media folder where I had all my photos stored. And I rummaged through photo after photo looking for pictures of family and friends who were smiling back at the camera. As soon as I had what I wanted, a picture of:

Mike, Jerry, Sam, myself, my parents, Mike's parents, and Heather's aunts, uncles and cousins, I exported the pictures into photo editing software I'd never used before, picked the collage format I wanted and then hit print. While I waited, with open hands, for the printer to complete its job and feed me the paper, the office light turned on, and I heard, "Jen?!"

In response, I turned and saw Mike in the office doorway. And I said, "Yeah?!"

He said, "What are you doing? It's like two or three in the morning. You know you have sleeping pills. From the looks of it, honey, you're not taking them are—"

As I caught the collage in my hands, I interrupted him and said, "I know. I'm sorry. I just had to do something. I'll be right to bed!"

"All right. We have an early morning so come on…"

"I'll be right there," I said.

Without saying another word, he left the office. But I didn't. Instead, I looked down at the collage in my hands, a collage with smiling faces that I wanted to give Heather so she wouldn't feel so alone while at the hospital. And then I broke down in tears and said, "What am I doing? Who am I trying to fool? I don't know what the hell to do!" And Death, lingering in the surrounding air, loved that I was floundering. He had what he wanted. My mind, body and soul were a mess. And now—I was easy prey. Though he tried, he couldn't take Heather. He failed at taking her life with the bite of a feral cat when she was a child. And he failed at taking her life with the poisonous drug concoction she took days earlier. So Death now questioned how he was going to take me. Would he take me by way of an accident or would he make me take my own life? With a weak *little* woman sitting at her desk crying as all hope seeped from her pores, he sat back and laughed a hearty laugh knowing she was his.

As Death laughed at me, I heard, coming from the office doorway, "I didn't think you'd listen to me. What's that in your hands?"

"It's just a picture I made for Heather. There's nothing on the walls in her hospital room. So I thought maybe this would cheer her up. I want her to see that her family loves her, Mike."

"Makes sense to me. You can take it to her in a few hours. Come on…let's get some sleep."

"I can't, Michael! If I give her this, she could try to kill herself again?!"

"I don't know what you mean?"

"I'm worried that if I give her this, she could feel like she has closure and will try to hurt herself again."

"I've never heard that before. But…I know what you mean. Do with it what you want. It's up to you. I think it's great. Let's get some sleep and talk about it when we get up."

I said, "Okay," and I followed him out of the room. But as I walked away from my desk, I crumpled up the collage and threw it in the garbage can and mumbled, "I'm not giving it to her. I can't." And we went to bed.

The second night she was on the seventh floor, Mike, Sam and I went to the hospital to visit with her during visiting hours. Upon our arrival at the nurses' station, and after we had signed in, emptied our pockets and showed the nurse a bag that had Heather's black sweatpants in it—without the string—a blue short sleeve tie-dyed shirt and brown leather flip-flops, we were allowed to enter the behavioral health unit. Just before heading through the automatic doors that had been unlocked for us, a nurse from behind a glass window pane said, "She's in the patient lounge."

I replied, "Okay…thank you."

The nurse responded by saying, "After you walk through the doorway, it's on your right."

I nodded and said, "Thanks."

We then walked to the patient lounge. When we walked into the room, I noticed that there was a small couch along the wall to my left, a TV in the opposite corner of the room and there were two picnic sized tables with chairs in the center of the room. On one table, I saw a light blue folder laying there labeled *Discharge Information*. It looked like someone had forgotten it. It was tangible proof that Heather wasn't alone on the seventh floor. I also saw a pamphlet labeled *Family and Visitor Guide* lying on another table. It was a reminder we were visitors.

After my eyes quickly scanned the room, I laid eyes on the most beautiful girl—my girl. She was sitting with another young lady who looked much younger than her. I'm not sure how old she was, but she looked like she was around the age of twelve. Even though Heather was busy talking to her peer, when we walked into the room, all three of us walked right up to her. I could tell that things were different. Heather appeared focused on what her new friend was saying. Regardless, we all three took turns embracing her. As we each took a turn and hugged her, we each said, "I love you!" before letting go of her. Once we got in our hugs, we walked over to the couch and sat down. There we were, Mike, Sam and I sitting on a couch like sardines in a sardine can.

With no wiggle room, we sat together watching our loved one, who didn't seem to know we were there. When Heather finally noticed us, she said, "Mom! Dad! Sam! Come here! I want you to meet someone!"

So we did as she said and got up from the minute couch we sat on and joined her and her friend at the table they sat at. And she introduced us to Rae. Rae was friendly. And she showed us a picture she had drawn of two blue cartoon characters. And then what happened next was bizarre. It was as if Heather forgot we were there. She refocused on Rae and conversed with Rae in a language we didn't understand.

Just then, Rae said, "No. You say it this way." And they continued to talk in a language we'd never heard before. From what we could gather, it was a language Heather's newfound friend made up. It was strange for us to see our twenty-year-old daughter conversing with the younger female patient, whom she had befriended, in a made up language.

Mike, Sam and I looked at each other with puzzled and concerned expressions. And then when visiting hours were over, we exited the room. Once out of earshot, I told Mike and Sam, "We have a problem."

They both nodded in agreement. And Mike said, "Things are worse than we thought." And with that, we left the hospital sadder and more lost than when we entered it. At that point, we could see our daughter had done damage to herself beyond what we could see on the outside of her body when she tried to snuff out her own life. The million dollar question was, "Just how much damage did she do?"

DISCHARGED

Forty-eight hours later, Mike, Jerry, Sam and I are sitting in the Jeep in the parking lot just outside the hospital's main entrance looking for Heather who had called me about a half hour earlier to tell me the doctor had discharged her. From the back of the Jeep, Sam says, "I don't see her!"

Jerry says, "I don't either!"

Mike joins the conversation and says, "Keep looking! She's here, guys."

While Mike and the kids continue to look for her, I see her. There she is...There's my girl...She's walking through the exit doors of the hospital dressed in the clothes I gave her a few days back. And even though she's covered in bruises, and her black sweatpants and blue tie-dyed shirt are hanging from her small frame, she looks beautiful. As I look at her in awe, the survivor she is, she's using her right hand to shield her eyes from the glare of the sun as she looks for us. And in this moment, if only for a second, something's right.

While I wait and watch for her to see us, the dark stage that the ballet dancer in the *Opera Show of Us* danced upon lights back up. But something appears to be wrong. The ballet dancer, with torn up bare feet and bloody toes—who dropped to her knees and buried her head within her hands as she cowered in the presence of what was—collapses on the old oak stage floor. And as she collapses, the stage goes dark once again.

Minutes pass, and then a click and a sparking sound rings out, and a single lightbulb lights back up and shines its unforgiving light on the ballet dancer whose damaged body lies motionless on the floor. The bright light from the bulb brightens and dims as the filament from within flitters and flicks and threatens to go out again. And as it does, something moves. It's her. And she's trying to get up. She pulls her disfigured body along the floor trying to get a grip on something. Then, with all of her might, she pushes herself up into a sitting position. And then...with her head down, and tucked between her chest and her knees, she curls her body up into a tight ball. And as she does, she pulls her feet up in pointe with only the tips of her damaged toes touching the floor in perfect ballet pose. And then...with only the strength a mother can find, with her head still down, she punches the sky with her right arm, and though shaky from the mad dance she's danced, she extends the *stained glass of* us, tight within her grip, high above her head.

Awakening

Jen, clutching the bronze French style ornate door handle with her left hand, nervously inserts the house key into the door lock above the handle with her right hand. She feels the weight of the glass storm door pressing against her backside as she attempts to keep the storm door open as she unlocks the house door. The key slides into the tumbler as the pins, one by one, align. As she twists the key to the right, she's flooded with feelings of deju vu. *It's okay. Take a deep breath. You've been here before, but this is Mom's house and Mom's doorknob. This isn't the doorknob to Heather's room. Exhale, Jen...*

She presses the lever of the door handle with her right thumb and pushes the door open. As the door gives way to the pressure of Jen's hand pushing against it, Jen walks hurriedly into the house shouting with uncertainty in her voice, "Mom?! Mom?! Where are you at?"

Silence.

The silence doesn't stop her. Instead, it pulls her in. She briskly walks into the kitchen again calling out, "Mom?!" She stops next to the dining room table and glances around the room. From the dining room, she can see that the living room is vacant. Without further hesitation, she runs down the hallway to the guest bedroom hollering, "Mom!" As she runs through the doorway, she sees her mom. She doesn't see the case yet that sits wide open next to her mom.

The bedroom walls, acting as a catapult, bounce the sound of her worried voice into the open space between the four walls, "Oh, Mom. Mom! Wake up!" Her mom, still in an upright position, doesn't wake up. Jen glances over at the case sitting next to her mom. She sees that it's open. With a puzzled look, she looks back at her mom. She sees the contents from the case on her mom's lap. She gently pushes on her mom's shoulder and says, "Mom? Are you okay? Mom?"

As Jen stares at her mother's sleepy face, she hears her mom gasp for air and then blurt out, "Oh! Jen?"

"Yes! It's me, Mom! It's all right. It's just me. Are you okay? I've been worried sick!"

"Yes! I'm okay. Where's your dad?!" says Jen's mom attempting to focus on Jen's face while blinking away the sleep in her eyes.

"He's still at the hospital. You didn't get my text messages, did you? The doctor has ordered more testing and won't release him yet. I took a taxi home so I can shower and get some different clothes on. What happened? What's going on?"

Jen's mom sits up and mutters, "I…I…I…oh no, Jen. I—"

Jen looks briefly at the open case and then back at her mom. "You didn't?"

"Uh…"

"Mom!"

"I'm so sorry, Jen. After we talked last night, I found myself in the guest room. And I've been…ohhhh, honey…I've been missing you terribly. You know, ever since Heather's last suicide attempt, I never hear from you. I know you must still be mad at me for leaving when Heather was still in the hospital. Things just haven't been the same since then!"

Jen looks away from her mom and takes a seat next to her on the bed. She stares at the dark hardwood floor. As the floor absorbs her fixated look, she inhales deeply and then lets out a sigh. She then turns her attention back on her mom and pointedly says, "You're right. I was mad and hurt. How could you do that? I told you I needed you!" Jen picks up the paperwork that comfortably lies on her mother's lap. "And now this?" Shaking her head in disappointment, she looks away from her mom and stares once again at the blameless floor.

"I didn't realize how sick she was, Jen. I'm so sorry. What I did was wrong. I can't explain it. All I can do is ask for your forgiveness...Jennnn...please, honey..."

The air, thick with guilt, becomes stale in the silence that once again exists. Emotions become hardened and suspended in time like ice crystals in a cirrus cloud. Time lapses for several seconds, seconds that seem like an eternity to Jen's mom. And then, Jen clears her throat and looks once again at her mom. With eyes, dripping with sorrow, she says, "Mom, I accept your apology. I'm so sorry."

"What?! Why are you sorry?! No!"

"I'm sorry that I disappeared! And you didn't know how sick Heather was."

"You don't have to explain!"

"Stop! Please. Just listen. I haven't been well ever since I found Heather. I got lost within myself. I mean, how does a person move forward after...all I could think about was... well you know what happened. I don't want to think about it right now. Remember yesterday when I asked you to remind me to tell you about the barn swallow I saw?"

"I do."

"Well, on the drive here, I hit one."

"You hit a barn swallow?"

"I did. And you know what?"

"What?"

"I thought I killed it! I mean, I was going like eighty miles per hour when it hit the grill! I just knew I killed it. And you know what was even worse?"

"What?"

"I couldn't stop! The traffic was too heavy! I had to keep going..."

"Oh, Jen."

"And then, you'll never believe what happened when I got to your house!"

"What happened?!"

"After I parked, I looked at the grill. I don't know why, but I had to."

"Yeah..."

"Mom! The bird was alive! It was alive! It flew out of the grill! I don't know how, but it did! It was amazing! And it even looked okay! I still can't believe it survived!"

"Oh my God! Honey!"

"Mom...Heather almost killed herself! I found her almost DEAD!"

Jen's mom sobs.

"It was *awful* when I found her. My beautiful girl was dying...and I couldn't stop what was already in motion. I couldn't save her! I know she's alive now, but that morning, my girl died. That precious baby girl I gave birth to all those years ago died. And in the moments that followed, after I found her on her bedroom floor, dying, life continued to happen all around me! I didn't want it to, but it did! I wanted to scream, 'STOP! We need help! We need help!' But I didn't."

"It's okay—"

"I had to keep going even though my girl was dying. I had to keep going...just like when I hit the bird...I couldn't stop. I had to call Mike to help us. I had to call 911. And the memories keep coming back...I relive it repeatedly! Like the barn swallow though, she got back up, Mom. She got up! She's alive! My girl's alive! But now I have a problem." Jen cries, "I'm scared...I'm so scared she'll succeed at killing herself."

"Have you talked to anyone about this?"

"Yes. The counselor I see said I have post-traumatic stress, post-traumatic stress! I thought only soldiers experienced that! I still am having a hard time believing I, Jennifer Stein, wife, mother, writer, producer...have PTSD! It makes sense though. Just when I think I've recovered, I see something that takes me back in time to those difficult days with Heather. And it's the most ridiculous things that can trigger a memory!"

"What things?"

"When I see a sandwich bag, I'm reminded that when Heather was taking classes, sometimes she'd forget to take her daily medication. So she'd call me and ask if I'd take them to her. I'd meet her on campus to deliver her a sandwich bag filled with her pills for the day in it. Mom! It was like I was carrying around her mental health in a bag, a sandwich bag! And then, like an avalanche, the memories from the day I found her in the basement flood my mind. And I fall again back into that black hole of psychological shock I fell into when I found her. A stupid sandwich bag has become a trigger! A gray t-shirt, like the one she was wearing when I found her, has become a trigger. An ambulance has become a trigger. I could go on and on! I see someone walking alone, and I remember that Heather's friends abandoned her while she was fighting for her life. Mom, they abandoned her. Can you believe it?"

"No! That's awful!" Jen's mom cries.

"And I felt like you left me the day you went back to the family reunion, Mom. I know that you didn't know what we were going through, but like the blue sparrow, and Heather, I was hit by something too. And I didn't know how to fly. I needed you to help me learn how to fly again. Mom...you told me I'd find a place to put it. Do you remember telling me that?"

"Yes."

"I've clung to those seven little words, Mom, as if they're a life raft keeping me afloat."

"What can I do to help?!"

"Listen. That's what I need. I need someone to listen."

"You've got it. I'm here now. I'm listening..."

"No one knows what Heather's been through. Did you know she developed involuntary muscle movements?"

"No! Was it a side effect?"

"Yeah. Her psychiatrist said it was from the antipsychotic she was taking. So he took her off of it and tried a different brand. It helped, but it took a while for the facial movements to stop and the muscle rippling she had elsewhere. Let's not talk about it. It's a trigger."

"You're right. Let's not and say we did."

"Thank you. So, Mom...your girl lives with PTSD. It's gotten better, but I still have issues. And what's really bizarre is no one talks about it. I know that there are other people affected by either their own struggles with mental illness or the mental illness of a family member. But they don't talk about it."

"You've got that right, Jen. But I think we've made strides. About a month ago, while I watched my favorite TV show, a *Breaking News* story interrupted the show."

"What was so important that your show got interrupted?"

"Law enforcement officials were trying to talk a teenage boy down from the clock tower at the high school. The building itself is five stories high. It was shocking to see him up there! I felt so helpless. I prayed that the young man would listen to the cops and come down off the roof."

"What happened? Did he?"

"He did. It took several hours though. But they got him to come down using the firetruck ladder. Later in the broadcast, a spokesperson from the police department reported that he had been hallucinating when he climbed up on the rooftop. From what I could gather, he heard voices, voices that told him to go to the top of the clock tower. The spokesperson said he lives with schizophrenia."

"Thank God he didn't get hurt!"

"I know! The young man—"

"Uh-huh—"

"He lives next door."

Jen leans in toward her mom and embraces her. And the two of them weep. The manuscript, nested safely between them, escapes the tears that flow. Then, Jen loosens her arms from around her mom and sits back on the bed. Her mom looks at her wondering what Jen will say next. Jen, pointing at the case says, "Do you not recognize the case?"

"Nooo…no…it seems familiar though."

"It was Grandmama's. You gave it to me when I was in high school. You really don't remember it?"

"It is? It is! I can't believe I forgot that?! My memory…it's been so sketchy lately."

"Oh, Mom! That's not good. We need to address this!"

"I know, dear. We will, but…the case…tell me more."

"Ever since you gave it to me, I've treasured it! And I blame you, you know, for my love of vintage luggage!"

Jen's mom smiles at Jen and says, "I'm so glad you're using it! It's a good thing you have it! I would have lost it!"

"Well, I stored Heather's medications in it after her second suicide attempt. I needed something that locked and looked inconspicuous so I used it for that. Isn't it interesting? I mean…it was the one piece of luggage that Grandmama was allowed to use when she was admitted to the hospital. Now that I think about it, you never told me why she was admitted to the hospital other than she had emotional problems. And you said she died there."

"Jen…we have so much to talk about."

"We do, Mom. I'm looking forward to it. It's interesting that I stored Heather's meds in it."

"It is. If this is where you stored her meds...where are they now?"

"She isn't taking medication anymore."

"What?!"

"Yeah! That's something I want to talk to you about later."

"Wow! I didn't expect to hear that!"

"I don't use the case for her meds anymore, but I still like to use it. It's a part of our story now. And it's a reminder to never forget what happened with Heather, and a reminder of how far we've come individually and as a family."

"Yes, honey!"

"Plus, there's something about the case that draws me to it. It's so special and dear to me because it was Grandmama's. This small piece of luggage is a reminder that there's a story to be told, a story about my Grandmama I can't wait to hear. Really...it's priceless." Jen points at the paperwork and asks, "Do you know what you read?"

"I think I do."

"The only way I could cope with Heather's illness, including her suicide attempts, was to write."

"That makes sense" says Jen's mom tenderly smiling and nodding her head.

"Does it?"

"I imagine that it gave you a sense of control..."

"Yes, but it's more than that though. How does a musical end? Many musicals, heck even books and movies, end happy like Annie and leave you with hope. I needed hope. One night, during Heather's recovery, while Mike was sleeping, I got up, went to my office and just wrote. The words poured out. From that night on, I wrote and I wrote, and before I knew it, I had written the story for my next musical, a musical I've titled *Stained Glass of Us*."

"Oh, Jen."

"I wanted you to read it first. That's why I came back home. I wanted to talk to you about Heather, and everything that's happened since, and share it with you before sharing it with Roland who's anxiously waiting for it."

"Really? I got to read it first?"

"Yes," Jen says, smiling and nodding her head at her mom. "Mom, I found hope!"

"If I may ask, how did you find hope, honey? *Stained Glass of Us* doesn't even have much of an ending, much less a happy ending."

"Exactly! The story doesn't end. It can't. Heather's mental illness hasn't magically gone away. It doesn't work like that. God how I wish it did, but it doesn't. *Stained Glass of Us* doesn't have a fairytale ending. But, as painful as it is, it breathes hope. And you know what else?"

"What?"

"While writing *Stained Glass of Us*, I got the feeling that there's *something* I'm supposed to do."

"Like what?"

"I don't know yet, but...we're not alone in this. Somewhere, at this moment, another family is feeling the impact of mental illness. There has to be a way I can help."

"Of course there is."

"Did I tell you I'm staying with you and Dad for a few weeks?"

"No!"

"Is that all right? I mean...I know I didn't tell you I was coming."

"Jen! Are you serious? Stop it! You know you don't have to ask. Did you tell your Dad yet?"

"Nope...not yet. I think today might be a good day to tell him! We sure have a lot of catching up to do, Mom. Did I tell you that Heather's singing again?"

"What?! No!"

Jen stands up and then helps her mom stand up. "How's your foot feeling this morning?"

Her mom carefully takes a step forward toward the guest-room doorway while holding onto Jen's arm and then stops. "Well…it doesn't hurt as bad!"

"Phew! That's good! But really! You need to call the podiatrist! I'll tell you what, while you make the call, I'll make coffee. I don't know about you, but I really need a cup. And we need to get back to the hospital and check on Dad. And Mom?"

"Yes?"

"Thank you."

"For what, dear?"

"For listening and being here for me. You're helping me fly again…"

A smile breaks loose across Jen's mom's face, and she gives Jen a bear hug. When she lets go of Jen, she says, "Did you say coffee?"

Jen, smiling at her mom, says, "You know it! Let's get it made. Oh! And tell me more about the young man next door. Have you talked to his parent's? How's he doing? And how are they doing?"

GLIMMER

He stands in his own driveway looking over the hood of his car at his neighbor's house. *Huh? That Jeep's still there. I wonder why I saw an ambulance last evening. And who's there? It couldn't be Jennifer Stein. She disappeared before anyone really got a chance to know her.*

And then he takes a step back and looks at his car, a marina blue 67' Camaro RS/SS Coupe. He wipes the sweat that now appears on his forehead with the back of his right hand. *Phew. This Indian summer weather!* He adjusts the round, chrome plated driver's side mirror. *I wish Josh was here to enjoy this moment with me. We finally got her done, son. She's yours, and you can't even drive her yet. Why? Why schizophrenia? What happened? What did I do to cause it?*

Deep in thought, he bends down and looks into the driver's side mirror. As he peers into the mirror, he has a flashback to the day he received the call that Josh was on top of the clock tower at the school. Time uncontrollably changes course and viciously reverses for him. Before he knows it, he's once again kneeling by the driver's side door of the Camaro.

The Camaro door is open, and he has the inside door panel off. He's busy installing the driver's side mirror. As he slides a washer on a bolt, his phone rings. He answers, "Yeah, this is Mr. Edwards. Say what? Oh my God! NO! I'm on my way!" His heart races as he relives the moment he learned Josh was on top of the school roof.

A warm gust of wind, out of nowhere, sideswipes him. He briefly, and quickly, shakes his head as the wind brings him back to reality. As he comes back to the present, he feels odd and out of place, and he's visibly shaken.

As he backs away from the mirror, and stands up, something catches his eye. He notices something near the front driver's side tire. His eyes focus on it. *What's that? How did I not see it?* He walks up to the tire and sees a piece of paper tightly adhered to the rubber as if it's glued to it. He kneels down on one knee in front of the tire. As his right knee connects with the concrete driveway, his knee immediately absorbs the warm heat that emanates from the hard surface. He braces himself with his left hand near the top of the fender and reaches for the piece of paper with his right hand. With his fingers, he gently grasps the edge of the paper and carefully pries it off.

Filled with curiosity, he stares at what looks like a piece of trash in his hands. And then he notices that the paper, once soaking wet but now partially dried, is torn at the top. He tries to make sense of the words near the top of the paper but to no avail. Last night's rainfall washed away most of the words. But one sentence near the bottom of the page clearly remains. And the four words and one period, in bold print that make up the sentence, look untouched as if the rain never happened at all. With eyes brimming with tears, and feelings of sadness, confusion and loneliness ravaging his body, he reads…**You are not alone.** He then hears the footsteps of someone approaching him. As he stands back up and looks across the hood of the Camaro, he sees a middle-aged woman with silver hair pulled up in a tight ponytail walking toward him. She says, as she extends her hand out for a handshake, "Sir? My name is Jennifer Stein!"

Note From The Author

When I wrote The Luggage Drop, I came to the table with firsthand knowledge about the effects of suicide and bipolar disorder because—I've been there. I was one of those "almost" left behind. The number of people affected by suicide, whether completed or not, is one too many.

Miraculously, Heather survived her suicide attempt, but it was an attempt that could have been prevented. Listed below is the National Suicide Prevention Lifeline toll-free number, a number I've shared with others and that may be helpful to you too or someone you care about. They also offer a chat service that you can access on their website.

You are not alone.

National Suicide Prevention Lifeline (24/7, free, confidential support): 1-800-273-8255
https://suicidepreventionlifeline.org/

P.S. You can find me at stacysflutterings.com where I list additional resources that have proven helpful for me and my family and that you might find helpful as well. There is good news. There is hope, and there are multiple resources and people available to help.

www.ingramcontent.com/pod-product-compliance
Lightning Source LLC
Chambersburg PA
CBHW031236260626
47169CB00007B/2317